D1388204

These are uncorrected proofs. All quotations or attributions should be checked against the bound copy of this book. We urge this for the sake of editorial accuracy as well as for your legal protection.

ISBN 1 84046 370 8

Joshua Cross
and the
Legends

Diane Redmond

WIZARD BOOKS

An imprint of Icon Books

Joshua Cross
and the
Legends

The Author

Diane Redmond is a broadcaster, television script writer, playwright and author with over a hundred and fifty titles to her name. Diane was born and educated in Lancashire. Her interest in children's books began in earnest when she was using them to teach English in language schools in Venice and Padua. She returned to England to live in Cambridge, where she taught multi-cultural education for several years before working as a radio and television presenter.

Her interest in the Ancient Greeks was awakened when she was asked to write *The Journey of Odysseus* for the Polka Children's Theatre in Wimbledon. After a successful run in London, the play toured East Anglia and was then commissioned by Penguin. *The Comic Strip Odyssey* was immediately followed by the publication of *The Greek Myths and Legends*, and later by another adaptation of *The Odyssey*.

Joshua Cross and the Legends has taken Diane deeper into the world of the Ancient Greeks. Here she examines the reality of their daily lives, the treatment of slaves, and the role of girls and women in society. She brings heroes, legends and the Immortals to life, entertaining us with the brilliance of philosophers, poets and mathematicians, and guiding us through the glory of the ancient Olympic Games.

The author would particularly like to thank Kate Agnew, an inspirational editor, and a powerhouse of knowledge and enthusiasm.

For my eldest daughter, Tamsin Tarling,

with all my love

Contents

CHAPTER ONE

Shakespeare's Chippy

Joshua Cross lives by the River Thames in London. Mrs Cross, his mum, runs a flourishing shop called Shakespeare's Chippy, situated between the London Eye and Waterloo Station. Shakespeare's Chippy is perfectly placed for hungry tourists visiting the South Bank and hungry patients visiting St Thomas's Hospital. Mrs Cross is famous the length of the Thames for her fried cod and crispy golden chips, which is fortunate for it is from the shop's proceeds that she supports her two sons and keeps a roof over their heads.

It hasn't always been so. As Tom, Josh's older brother by six years, never fails to tell him, family life was brilliant until he came into existence. Then they'd lived in a big house further downriver, near Greenwich. Their garden ran right down to the Thames, where Mr Cross kept a rowing boat moored to the bank. He often rowed his wife and son along the river, until one warm summer night, just as the moon was rising and nightingales were filling the air with their liquid song, he stood up to swap places with Tom and suddenly fell overboard. Knowing he could swim like a fish, his wife and son had waited for him to bob back to the surface, but tragically he never did. Alexander Cross, sea captain and father of two, disappeared under the fast-flowing waters of the Thames and his body was never found. It didn't float out on the tide at Gravesend, neither did it get washed upstream to Docklands and Canary Wharf. Mr Cross just disappeared off the face of the earth and the shock of it sent Mrs Cross, who was seven months pregnant, into premature labour. Joshua was born, pronounced virtually dead and placed in an incubator where, wired up to bleepers in St Thomas's antenatal intensive care unit, he lay suspended between life and death for two months. Then on June 21st, the day he should have been born, he re-entered life kicking and screaming.

During Joshua's stay in St Thomas's, his family were evicted from their grand house in Greenwich and his mother, demented at the loss of a beloved husband, realised she would have one son, perhaps two, to feed. Before she'd married Alexander Cross she'd run an upmarket restaurant near Tower Bridge; now she could only afford a lock-up shop with accommodation. So she opened Shakespeare's Chippy, the only home Josh has ever known. By the age of five, he was an old hand at mixing batter, chopping chips, gutting fish, heating meat pies and cooking mushy peas.

Everyday before he leaves for school, he refills the salt and vinegar bottles dotted around the shop and rips up newspaper for his mum to wrap the steaming bags of fish and chips in.

Every night, with the smell of frying chips drifting through their open bedroom window, Josh begs his big brother to tell him again about the father he never knew.

'He looked like you but he was tall. Really tall, about six foot four. He had blond hair that was almost silver and silvery-grey eyes, like summer rain. He was always smiling and telling jokes. He was strong too. He could pick up an armchair with me in it and run around the room holding it. He knew about other countries and different religions. He knew the names of the stars and where the oceans met. He could speak five different languages and had travelled round the world eight times.'

Joshua smiles as he snuggles down to sleep. He's heard these things many times but he stills likes to hear them said out loud. He closes his eyes and snuggles under his duvet, proud of his father whose silvery-grey eyes he never knew.

Joshua goes to St Mary's Primary School on the banks of the Thames. It's a rambling red-brick Victorian building straight opposite the Houses of Parliament. 'The school's rubbish, but the view's got to be one of the best in London,' Josh's best friend Stevie always jokes. Josh's other best friend is Dido, an eleven-year-old girl with a brain the size of the planet! She knows *everything*, she always wins the prizes, she's teacher's pet – and remarkably she's still their friend!

It was football not intellect that brought them together.

For years they've played in the same team: Dido in centre-forward, Stevie left-back and Josh on the wing. They are an inseparable threesome who couldn't look more different. Josh is small, pale and skinny with blond hair and silver-grey eyes. Stevie is tall, dark, athletic and the best long-distance runner in the school. Dido is head-and-shoulder taller than Stevie and towers over Josh. She has a mass of long golden-red hair, a face full of freckles and eyes so blue Josh sometimes feels dizzy just staring into them.

When Josh and Stevie first met Dido they burst out laughing when they heard her name.

'You're not really called Dido Cleopatra Dudah?' giggled cheeky Stevie.

Dido nodded. 'My Lebanese dad gave me the name but didn't hang around long enough for mum to get the spelling. He ran off as soon as I was born.'

'Aren't parents great?' said Stevie. 'All I want to do is run in the Olympic Games and my dad wants me to train as a chartered accountant!'

'My mum's OK,' Josh said staunchly.

'Yeah but what about your old man drowning two months before you were born?' joked Stevie. 'Inconsiderate or what!'

In their final year at St Mary's School Josh and Stevie would have been recorded as congenital idiots if it hadn't been for Dido. Nobody knew whether it was her Lebanese dad or her Irish mum, who worked as a ward sister at St Thomas's hospital, who Dido inherited her IQ from. She knew the answers to all the maths questions. She could knock out an essay easy as breathing. She could draw maps with her eyes shut, she could recall the names of all the capital cities and she corrected their science homework every Monday on their way to school. Dido knew *everything* and they knew nothing, which is why it was so strange when Josh suddenly became the world's expert on Ancient Greek! It was a subject he might have liked if he'd taken the trouble to learn about it. From the books he'd flicked through he liked the sound of their civilisation – the sun-soaked landscape, the sailing ships, the architecture, the Olympics, and, best of all, those vengeful gods and blood-curdling monsters! But if it was a choice between going to the library to brush up on his Greek or knocking a football round the playground, then football won every time.

CHAPTER TWO

The London Eye

It all starts with a dream. A dream where he's walking through meadows knee-deep in wild flowers. As he brushes past them an intense perfume drifts up and saturates his senses. Dazed by its sweetness he stops and looks around. Then he sees a man and knows it is Alexander Cross, his father. He's wearing silver armour and his hand rests on a sword hanging in its scabbard from his belt. He walks towards Joshua speaking urgently.

'You're in grave danger, my son. A man who is my enemy is trying to kill you.'

'Who is he?' Josh asks.

'His name is Leirtod. He is coming to find you.'

The dream fades and Joshua wakes with a strange sense of unease. The dream was so real and his father seemed really frightened – but why would anybody want to kill him? And who's Leirtod, Josh wonders as he hurries downstairs to help his mum before he leaves for school.

'Did my dad have any enemies?' he asks Mrs Cross as he pours a bucket of peeled potatoes into the chip-chopping machine.

'Enemies?' she cries as she briskly whisks the fish batter. 'You must be joking. Everybody loved your dad – *everybody*!'

'Where do you think he is now?' Josh asks.

Mrs Cross stops mixing and a smile flickers on her lips. 'Your dad's in heaven.'

'Do people in heaven wear silver armour?'

She looks thoughtful as she dips fillets of fish into the creamy batter. 'Heroes might,' she replies then she looks at him and says proudly, 'Your dad was a hero.'

Josh goes out into the yard to bring in another bucket of potatoes. As he stoops to pick it up he sees something out of the corner of his eye. Looking up he catches sight of a tall figure in a black cloak running out of the back gate. Dropping the bucket he runs after the figure who is hurrying down the side street towards the river. Josh watches him leap aboard a boat with a red sail, which swoops off at great speed down the Thames. Mystified he hurries home and tells his mum there was somebody snooping around the yard.

'Maybe it was one of those tramps who sleep rough on the embankment,' she says unconcerned. Josh doesn't want to alarm her by saying that the man took off in a sailing boat!

'Be careful,' he says anxiously as he leaves for school.

'I'm always careful,' she replies as she gives him a kiss and sends him on his way.

As usual Dido's waiting for Josh on the towpath by the London Eye.

'It's Monday,' he moans. 'Give us a hand with my home-work!'

'What do you want first, duh-brain, the maths answers or the science graph?'

'Both!'

'Don't you ever do any work?'

'I don't need to with a genius like you around.'

Dido holds her hand out for his maths book which he proffers but she doesn't take it.

'Don't look now,' she whispers. 'But I think somebody's following you.'

Josh's blood runs cold. 'Is it a guy in a long black cloak?'

Dido nods.

'He was hanging around the shop this morning,' says Josh. 'I thought he'd gone away.'

Dido shakes her head. 'He didn't go far!'

'Let's lose him,' says Josh as he breaks into a run. Years of chasing a ball around a football pitch have made the pair of them very fit and very fast. They tear down the towpath, dodging around trees and lamp-posts, avoiding joggers, cyclists and mothers with toddlers. They dart down alley-ways and run up side streets until eventually they lose him.

'He's gone,' says Dido as she peers around a corner and sees that the towpath is empty.

'Thank goodness for that,' gasps Josh and then they hear the sound of galloping hooves and the ground shakes beneath their feet.

'It's a stampede!' screams Josh as he pulls Dido behind a garden wall.

They crawl under some bushes and kneel down. Sharp gravel cuts into their knees but neither of them move as a mighty thundering noise passes so close it lifts the hair on the top of their heads. As it recedes Josh nervously peers out.

'What can you see?' asks Dido.

Speechless with amazement he can only shake his head.

'Was it an elephant?'

'NO.'

'A rhino?'

'No ... it was a sort of horse!' he says faintly.

'Don't be daft! A horse couldn't possibly make all that noise.'

'It was a *monstrous* centaur ...' His voice trails away in disbelief.

'Centaur? Since when did you know about centaurs?'

'Since NOW!' he replies impatiently. 'It's a mythical beast from Ancient Greece with the body of a horse and the chest, arms and head of a *man* – this one had sharp tufts of hair, like horns!'

Dido looks at him with an expression that is a mixture of both fear and awe. 'You're winding me up, aren't you, Josh?'

'I *saw* it, Dido.'

'And it looked like a centaur?'

'It didn't look like one, it *was* one,' he insists angrily.

'OK, I believe you,' she says quickly. 'All we've got to do now is work out why a mythical beast is running up and down the Thames Embankment?'

'I don't know,' Josh replies. 'But it scared me to death!'

Throughout the day Joshua is uneasy. He can't settle to anything, not even a game of football at lunchtime. When Stevie hears about the spooky man and the centaur he bursts out laughing.

'Oh, yeah!'

'I saw them!' Josh exclaims.

Stevie turns to Dido. 'And what did you see, Snow White and the Seven Dwarves?'

'It's not funny, Stevie. The man was like a demon.'

Stevie dribbles the ball at his feet. 'Maybe it was somebody on their way to a fancy-dress party,' he says, then adds impatiently, 'Come on, let's have a game before the bell goes.'

The school day finishes with a double history lesson. Mr Wilkinson their teacher, who they call Fingers because he spends most of his time picking his great cavernous nose, hangs a map of Ancient Greece over the blackboard. Joshua stares at it, intrigued by the many islands dotted around the ancient Aegean sea: Seriphos, Delos, Paxos, Naxos, Samos, Skyros. He wonders if monstrous centaurs inhabit any particular one? Fingers has a satisfying delve into his left nostril then begins.

'The Ancient Greeks worshipped a number of Gods,' Fingers starts. 'The most powerful of them is Zeus, who has two brothers and two sisters.'

'Three sisters actually,' says Josh before he can stop himself.

Stevie and Dido gape at Josh like he's split the atom. Josh gapes back at them, more astonished than they are. Fingers blinks in disbelief.

'*Three sisters*, Cross? Are we absolutely sure about that?' he says in a voice that is loud with ridicule.

Joss vehemently nods his head. 'Demeter, Hera and Hestia.'

'Wow, Josh!' Dido exclaims. 'First it's centaurs now it's the gods.'

Josh doesn't know what to do. His brain is humming with knowledge – and it's all about Ancient Greece! He can understand their language, he knows their history, he can almost taste their food! What's going on? Has a deranged Greek spirit taken possession of his football-saturated brain?

'Who knows the names of Zeus's brothers?' Fingers asks as his eyes sweep around the room.

'Don't look at me,' Stevie jokes. 'Ask my mate Joshua Feta Cheese here!'

The class laugh at Stevie's joke but Josh doesn't hear it. The names Poseidon and Hades are ringing round his head. He forces himself to be silent and Dido provides the answers.

'Poseidon and Hades,' she replies.

'But there were old gods before Zeus and his brothers and sisters,' Josh blurts out.

'Man, oh man! Did your mum mix brain fodder in with your Corn Flakes this morning?' gasps Stevie in astonishment.

Josh desperately wants to stop talking but the words simply won't stop coming out of his mouth. 'The old gods were Cronus and Rhea who were protected by a guard of Titans. Rhea gave birth to lots of children but Cronus always swallowed them alive!'

'I wish somebody had done that with my kid sister,' jokes Stevie. 'She never stops bawling.'

'When baby Zeus was born Rhea hid him in a cave but Cronus demanded to see the child so Rhea wrapped a large stone in swaddling clothes and presented it to Cronus who swallowed it whole!'

'So now Cronus has got SIX baby gods in his stomach!' Dido chips in excitedly. 'Meanwhile Zeus is growing up fast so Rhea gets him a job as cup bearer to Cronus. Zeus mixes his dad a drink and puts a potion in it which makes him violently sick.'

With relish Joshua takes up the tale. 'First Cronus throws up the stone he swallowed then he vomits up Zeus's brothers and sisters, all unharmed.'

'Unharmed but totally covered in sick. Great!' scoffs Stevie. 'Then what?'

'Hades, Poseidon and Zeus fought Cronus and his Titan guards,' says Josh. 'And Zeus struck his father down with a thunderbolt.'

'Would either of you mind if I got a word in edgeways?' asks Fingers who's looking slightly put out. 'I am the teacher here, after all.'

Josh blushes and wriggles self-consciously in his seat. Dido is much more forthright.

'Are you going to tell us about the hierarchy of the new gods?'

'Er, no,' he replies in a startled voice. 'I was moving on to the story of Odysseus.'

'Oh, but you *must* explain what happened to Zeus and his brothers and sisters,' she insists.

'Must I … ?' he mutters.

She nods her head and explains for him!

'With Cronus and Rhea out of the way Zeus settled on what the Immortals thought was the highest mountain in the world, Mount Olympus. Hades went down into the Underworld where he ruled over the shadows of the dead, Poseidon became ruler of the seas, Demeter was goddess of the harvest and Hestia assumed the minor role of goddess of the hearth – symbol of the home and family – and was hardly ever heard of again! Zeus married his sister Hera and had many children, some by her and *lots and lots* by beautiful mortal women who he seduced—'

'Enough of that Dido!' snaps Fingers.

'Why stop at the good bits?' chuckles Stevie.

Fingers snappily taps the map of Ancient Greece with his ruler.

'Moving swiftly on. This is Ithaca.'

'My auntie went there with Thomsons last summer,' says Stevie.

'She got sunburnt on the first day and was indoors for a week!'

'Well, I'm sure Odysseus didn't have that problem,' says Fingers. Trying to regain their attention he waves towards the map. Joshua's eyes are drawn to it like a magnet. To his amazement a school of silver dolphins leap up and bound through the shimmering, blue Mediterranean sea. A seagull screeches. Startled Joshua turns to see one perched on the windowsill. The bird cocks his head as if examining him then flies off. Josh watches its flight across the school play-ground where it circles above the demonic man who's now astride the centaur! Crying out in fear Joshua leaps to his feet.

'Ahhh! It's him!'

'What's got into you, boy?' shouts Fingers.

'There's a centaur in the playground!'

The entire class bursts out laughing.

'What's a centaur when it's at home?' laughs one of the girls.

'It's a mythical beast – half man, half horse – and it's *out there*!' Josh yells.

As a body the class rise to their feet and stare out of the window in the direction of Josh's trembling finger. All they see is an empty playground but there is a distant sound of galloping hooves. Josh blinks as if waking from a dream.

'It's gone …' he murmurs in confusion.

22

By now Fingers has had it.

'That's it, Cross. One way or another you've taken over the history lesson so now you can conclude it. Tell us about Odysseus and the Trojan War – *now*!'

Fingers glares at him, waiting to hear him say, 'I can't, sir.' But he can! With his new wealth of Ancient Greek knowledge on tap he begins the story.

'Odysseus and other Greek Kings went to war with Menelaus because a Trojan guy called Paris had nicked Menelaus's wife, Helen, who was thought to be the most beautiful woman in the world. Agamemnon, who was Menelaus's brother, led the entire Greek army to the city of Troy where they fought the Trojan army for *ten years*. Loads and loads of Greeks died outside the gates of the impenetrable city. They were all on the point of giving up and going home to their families when Odysseus came up with the brilliant idea of building an enormous wooden horse, which a specially chosen band of warriors would hide inside.'

'Pity he didn't have that brainwave ten years earlier, it would've saved a lot of mucking about!' jokes Stevie.

'Odysseus figured it was a starter for ten if some of them were *inside* Troy rather than all of them *outside*!' Josh explains.

Not convinced Stevie asks, 'How could Odysseus be sure that the Trojans would take the wooden horse into their city?'

'He couldn't be sure – it was a cunning, calculated risk.'

Josh looks around the class to see if he's boring everybody sideways but they're all hanging on his every word!

'Go on, boy!' urges Fingers excitedly.

'So they built the horse and late at night they dragged it to the gates of the city with the warriors inside. At dawn the Trojan lookout saw the huge horse and alerted the guard who called the war generals. From the city wall they stared at the giant horse and decided it was a gift from the gods. They hauled it into the heart of the city where all the townspeople celebrated the gods' gift by throwing a party that went on all day and all night. Inside the belly of the horse the Greeks could hear people singing and rejoicing – they could also hear them getting blind drunk! They waited until the Trojans were fast asleep then they opened the gates to the rest of the army who slaughtered every Trojan they laid eyes on. By dawn the city was running in blood and Troy was burnt to the ground.'

'Wow! Those Ancient Greeks don't do things by halves, do they?' gasps Stevie.

'After ten long years of war the Greeks could finally go home.' Joshua pauses dramatically. 'But it took Odysseus another ten years to get home.'

'What happened – did he get lost?' asks Stevie.

'They got lost *big time*,' Josh tells him. 'Poseidon was furious with Odysseus for destroying Troy so he blew him and his men around the seas of the world for ten years. He fought witches, monsters and demons, he even visited the Underworld, but finally Athene persuaded her brother to let him go home and Odysseus sailed back to Ithaca.'

Joshua finishes his gripping yarn and the entire class, led by Fingers, give him a standing ovation which makes him blush crimson with embarrassment. As the bell rings for the end of school he dashes out of the gates keen to avoid everybody, but Dido and Stevie chase after him.

'Hey, wait for us, Brain of Britain!' Stevie hollers.

'What's got into you?' asks wide-eyed Dido. 'I start off the day by doing your homework and end it listening to you talking about the Ancient Greeks like you were doing a degree in it! You were brilliant, Josh!' she raves.

'I thought you were thick like me!' laughs Stevie as he starts pressing buttons on his mobile phone. 'But you're a genius so I'm entering you for "Who Wants to be a Millionaire" *right now.*'

'NO!' cries Josh in alarm. 'It's not me that's doing the talking. Somebody else is.'

'Maybe I can enter whoever he or she might be!'

'I don't know what's happening to me,' mutters Josh miserably.

Dido suddenly stops in her tracks and goes deathly pale. 'He's back!' she gasps.

The three of them turn and see the demonic man on the towpath. He glares at them and they reel under the impact of a violent force drilling into their skulls. He snarls and raises his arm as if to strike them but his arm freezes in mid-air as if blocked by an invisible power. His eyes dilate and a red laser-like beam flashes from them.

'RUN!' yells Stevie.

Like terrified rabbits they scatter, but their pursuer is everywhere – in front, behind and all around them – blocking their every move.

'Get on the Eye!' screams Dido.

The four-hundred-and-fifty-foot tall, turning wheel is right ahead, surrounded by hundreds of tourists all patiently waiting their turn in a long queue. The three terrified children jump the queue by leaping over the barriers and running headlong up the ramp pursued by angry security guards. The girl directing people into the passenger capsules gapes in astonishment as she sees three kids running wildly towards her.

'No! Get back!' she shouts as they jump into the capsule which has one old lady in it.

'Oh, isn't this wonderful?' enthuses the old lady as the door sweeps shut and the capsule slowly rises. Breathless with relief the children slump on the wooden bench in the middle of the carriage and look around.

'Have we lost him?' asks Dido.

'I can't see him,' says Stevie, glancing into the capsule rising up behind them.

Josh looks up to the capsule in front and goes white with shock. The man is above them! Through the clear perspex window he can see his black cloak billowing out around him. It floats out like a dark storm cloud obscuring the views of Westminster and the South Bank.

'He's a monster!' gasps Stevie, faintly.

'He's my father's enemy and he wants to kill me,' whispers Joshua as the horrifying realisation hits him like a chilling premonition.

Slowly their capsule reaches its apex giving breathtaking views of the Thames, the City and the East End.

'Oooh, there's St James Park and Buckingham Palace,' raves the old lady as she dashes around the capsule pointing out the landmarks.

The children don't look at the dramatic panorama unfolding below them. They are mesmerised by the man who is clearly invisible to her. As the Eye reaches its highest point he suddenly switches carriages! First he's behind, then overhead, then in front and underneath them. The children gaze in horror as he leaps from carriage to carriage, leering at them like a taunting demon. As the wheel starts its slow descent and Big Ben and the Houses of Parliament swing into view Joshua asks the question that's on all their minds.

'What're we going to do when this thing stops?'

Their capsule is moving towards the landing pad where a group of angry security guards are waiting to grab them. Fortunately the old lady forms a perfect shield between the children and the guards.

'*Marvellous!*' she cries as the doors swing open. The children dodge around the guards' grasping hands and tear through the crowd. Once on the towpath they disappear into the familiar network of streets behind St Thomas's hospital.

'SPLIT!' yells Stevie as he runs off.

Dido darts off to the right and Joshua heads for home, running like the devil were at his heels.

Josh reaches Shakespeare's Chippy where a long queue is forming for the teatime opening. Knowing his mum will be needing him in the shop he hurries round to the back door which he opens then stops, rooted to the spot, as he smells rank breath on his neck. He turns and looks into the face of the man. It is the face of evil. White as death with eyes like pinpoints of glittering hatred. The man reaches out to grasp Joshua's shoulder but he stiffens; again some force seems to be stopping his hand. He scowls then suddenly bursts into bitter laughter.

'Your father is protecting you today but this is his last day. Tomorrow I will have the son of Lumaluce.' His words ring out as the ground shakes under Joshua's feet. 'Enjoy your last night in this life, boy!'

The sound of galloping hooves thunders by and he's gone. With his skin crawling in terror Joshua darts into the shop and huddles close beside his mother who is busy frying fish and chips.

'Give us a hand, love,' she says. 'Bring in the mushy peas and start refilling the vinegar bottles.'

On automatic pilot Josh does as he's told but he doesn't stray far from her side and jumps in fear every time anybody in a dark coat walks into the shop. At closing time Mrs Cross tucks Joshua up in bed and gives him a big hug.

'Sweet dreams,' she says. 'And wake up happy on your birthday.'

Joshua falls into a deep sleep haunted with dreams … Mist rises as the sun breaks over the sea, turning it wine dark. Seagulls follow a red-sailed boat with a single bright eye painted on each side of the prow. His father is standing in the stern waving to him. The early morning light glancing off his silver armour dazzles Josh's eyes.

'Come, Joshua. I'll take you on a journey.'

'But dad, I thought you were dead.'

'Nobody dies, my son. I have always been with you.'

'Dad, I'm scared. There's a man following me. He says he's going to kill me tomorrow, on my birthday.'

'His name is Leirtod. He will succeed if I don't remove you.'

'Why does he want to kill ME?'

'He has vowed to destroy my heir.'

Josh was going to say, 'But what about Tom, he's your heir too?' but his father interrupts him.

'I have been able to protect you for ten years but in your second decade of life you will have to defend yourself. My power has so far been greater than Leirtod's, but as you approach manhood his strength grows over mine. I cannot protect you here in the present but I can hide you in the past.'

Joshua wants to ask a thousand questions but a sea mist rises and obscures his father's face.

'Dad, I'm scared. Don't leave me.'

'We will meet in the past,' his father calls. 'I will be waiting for you, Joshua.'

A seagull screeches over the sound of the waves and Joshua wakes up in his own bed with his duvet in a knot around his head. Gasping in fear he peeps out expecting to see Leirtod hovering over him. Nobody's there. He lowers the duvet and listens to the familiar morning sounds – his mother clattering around in the shop downstairs, his brother yelling as he squeezes his spots in the bathroom.

Everything's OK, he tells himself. It was just a bad dream. He throws his duvet off and walks towards the door but his legs buckle beneath him. Groaning he crawls back to bed and lies down but the bed feels like it's rolling through waves as high as the house. The taste of salt water fills his mouth. 'UGHHH!' he gags as he dashes to the bathroom where he's violently sick.

'Happy Birthday!' says Tom as they pass each other on the landing.

'I've just been sick,' says Joshua feebly.

'Right, any excuse to skive off school!' his brother replies.

Feeling queasy Josh makes his way downstairs where he finds Mrs Cross in the back shop swiftly gutting fresh fish. Decapitated heads with bulging eyes lie beside silvery guts spilling blood and entrails in an enamel bucket. Joshua's stomach heaves and he dashes for the toilet.

After he's been violently sick for the second time in five

minutes Josh staggers into the kitchen where he's startled by a loud screech. Perched on the windowsill, pecking at the glass with a hard yellow beak, is a great big seagull.

'It's you!' cries Josh as he recognises the bird he saw at school the previous day. The bird cocks its head and taps against the window.

'*AWKK*!'

Suddenly the call of seabirds fills the kitchen and Joshua feels a warm breeze brush the hairs on the back of his neck. The seagull squawks impatiently and flaps its wing.

'Oi, mate, what do you want?'

The bird winks at him and flies off. Josh runs outside to watch it go but bumps into the postman who shoves a card into his hands. As he tears open the envelope Joshua notices the stamp – it's not a picture of the Queen's head. It's a silver dolphin slicing through pale blue waves. He's never seen such a lovely stamp ... the card is lovely too. A picture of a coastline surrounded by white sand and blue sea. It looks like paradise. There's no message, no name. Maybe a girl fancies him? Joshua's stomach flips, though not with excitement – the sickness has come back. Keen to avoid going back into the shop and seeing the bulging eyes of dead fish he calls goodbye to his mum and sets off along the towpath where he meets up with Dido and Stevie.

'WOSSSSUUUP!' bellows Stevie as he shoves a Crunchie bar into Josh's hand. The sight of the chocolate bar makes Joshua go pea-green.

'Ugh, I feel seasick.'

Stevie bursts out laughing. 'Don't be daft. We're only walking by the Thames we're not sailing on it!'

Dido cautiously checks the towpath. 'I don't think we're being followed today,' she says with obvious relief.

Josh sticks his hands deep into his pockets and mumbles, 'I don't know what's happening to me.'

'That's what happens when you turn eleven,' says Stevie cheerfully. 'All the troubles of the world land on your shoulders!'

'Just kick me if I start blabbing about the Ancient Greeks again.'

'No chance!' says Dido. 'It was the best history lesson we've ever had and you were a STAR!'

'But I don't want to be a star! I like being boring and stupid and not feeling sick and scared all of the time.'

Dido raises her blue eyes in disgust. 'You boys are so stupid! Just when you're getting to be really interesting you try to regress.'

'What's regress?' asks Stevie.

'Go back to what you were before you were interesting,' she says.

'Well I think I'm regressing to Ancient Greece,' Josh tells them. 'I'm even dreaming about it.'

Once in school, Josh has no sudden bursts of inspiration. A combination of queasiness and exhaustion send him into a trance. He stares sleepily at the map left hanging on the blackboard from yesterday's history lesson. Suddenly he can hear the shushing sound of the sea and waves start to break around the land mass called the Peloponnese. Dolphins spring up and leap through the waves, their silver bodies twisting and turning, iridescent silver in the bright sunshine. Seabirds screech over the roar of the ocean, then a gigantic wave forms and thunders out of the map, filling the classroom, swallowing up the school and sweeping him along.

'Stevie! Dido! Help me!' he screams as he goes under ...

CHAPTER THREE

The Sightless Seer

Josh is flung down to an ocean bed lined with the pale skeletons of the long dead. Salt water fills his lungs; his eyes bulge; his lungs ache. He's drowning.

'Ride the wave, Joshua,' his father's voice calls over the roaring sea.

He takes a deep breath and dives through the wave, which propels him forward at an amazing speed. He surfaces, weak and breathless, but he's on land, gazing at a coastline … *exactly* like the picture on the birthday card he received that morning. He gets to his feet and stands in the shallows looking around, but the blazing sun and scorching white beach dazzle him. He covers his eyes against the glare, then hears DING … DING … DING … DING. He looks up and sees an old, stooped man dressed in rags. He dodders towards Joshua, clasping a bell in his gnarled hand.

'Boy, is that you?' he calls tremulously.

Josh neither speaks nor moves. He stands facing the old man who walks straight past him. As he passes, Josh sees his eyes which are white and sightless. He's blind – he can't see him. The old man suddenly stops and sniffs the air like a dog.

'Boy! Answer me!'

Josh doesn't know what to say. He gulps and blurts, 'Er, hello!' like they'd just bumped into each other in Tesco!

The old man reaches out and grasps Joshua. He presses the bones of his face and head then pushes open his mouth to feel his teeth. Wriggling uncomfortably, like a dog at the vet's, Josh wonders what the old man is up to. Finally he stops and nods.

'Yes, you have the same skull as Lumaluce. Follow me!'

He scurries barefoot across the scorching-hot beach. Josh, who's lost his shoes in the sea, hops and yelps as he follows him into a cool cave where a rivulet flows across the sandy floor. Glad to be out of the scorching heat Joshua flops to the ground, but the old man barks, 'Get up boy. I have a task for you.'

Josh is startled by his tone. Not even his mum speaks to him like that when she wants two buckets of potatoes carrying in from the yard. Before he can stop himself the word 'Why?' is out of his mouth.

'Joshua Cross, I am about to set you off on a journey that will lead you to your father. You will do as I say, or I shall not give you the means to begin your odyssey.' As he speaks he places two terracotta jugs before Joshua. 'Here is a five-litre jug and a three-litre jug. I want you to measure out exactly *four litres*.'

Joshua gapes at him in utter disbelief – he's *the worst* pupil in his class at maths and this old guy wants him to perform a four-litre miracle.

'I can't!'

Though blind the old man glares at him from his unseeing eyes.

'It is not for the son of Lumaluce to say "*I can't*!" This is the first test on your journey. You must THINK, boy!'

Josh hasn't a clue but he knows he's got to appease the old man, otherwise he might never get out of the cave. He grabs the largest terracotta jug and dips it into the stream. It's heavy when it's full to the brim but he manages to carry it back to the old man without spilling more than a few drops. 'OK, there's five litres,' he says without a clue what to do next. 'Got any good ideas?' he asks persuasively.

'From the five-litre jug fill up the three-litre jug', he replies.

With effort Josh lifts the heavy jug and fills up the smaller three-litre jug.

'Now I've got two litres left in the big jug,' he says.

'Leave it there and empty out the three-litre jug you've just filled.'

Josh does as he's told, wondering all the time how he's going to measure out another two litres of water to go with the two he's already got.

'Pour the two litres in the big jug into the small jug and fill the five-litre jug again,' the old man says.

Staggering under the weight of the water in the heavy terracotta pot, Josh plonks it down on the ground and awaits further instructions.

'Now you must think for yourself, Joshua Cross!'

He looks from one jug to the other. 'I've got five litres

in the big jug and two litres in the three-litre jug,' he mutters. 'How do I get four?'

Suddenly the penny drops. 'YES! YES!' he yells. 'If I pour another litre of water into the smaller jug there'll only be four left in the big one!'

He quickly pours off enough water to top up the smaller jug then turns to the old man with a big grin on his face.

'I've done it!'

'Good. Now I will tell you my name,' says the old man. 'I am Tiresias, the seer.'

'What's a seer?'

'I am a holy prophet in what you call Ancient Greece.'

'I'm in Ancient Greece!' gasps Josh. 'Lumaluce *really* did send me back in time!'

'Of course. How else could he protect you from Leirtod?'

'You know him too?'

Tiresias nods. 'I have seen him, though he does not appear to ordinary mortals.'

'He appeared to me and my friends in broad daylight!'

'He *wanted* you to see him,' Tiresias replies.

'So I wasn't dreaming about my father last night – it was *real*?'

'Of course it was real,' snaps the old man impatiently. 'Your father was preparing you for the start of your journey.'

'Is he in heaven? Is that where I'm going?'

'Your father, Lumaluce, is light itself. He has bathed in

the river of life and visited the sky's vault. He lives in a state of permanent happiness in the Fields of Joy, a place beyond Hades which we call the Underworld.'

'Do I have to die to get there?'

'You may die if Leirtod gets to you,' Tiresias replies briskly. 'If you develop your intellect and use the gifts that will be given to you on your journey, you may outwit him.'

Keen to get started Joshua asks, 'How do I get to these Fields of Joy?'

Tiresias lays a warning hand on his shoulder.

'In order to get to the Fields of Joy, you have to travel down to Hades and enter the Underworld. It is a long and dangerous journey, son of Lumaluce. *If* your journey is successful,' he chillingly stresses the word '*if*', 'I will be waiting for you on the banks of the River Styx.

'You will need this,' he adds as he hands Joshua a coin. 'Charon the Ferryman will not row you over the river if you do not pay his fare. You will also need this.'

This time he hands Joshua a little leather purse, which he slips into his pocket along with the coin.

'The purse contains white barley which you will need to use before you make your crossing to the Underworld.'

Mystified, Josh asks, 'What do I do with it?'

'A great hero will tell you exactly what to do with it. Listen carefully to his words or you will die.'

Utterly confused and pretty terrified, Joshua asks, 'Where am I now?'

'You are on the island of Zachynthus,' Tiresias replies as

38

he bustles him out of the cave. 'From here take a boat to Elis. There you will be guided by another. Farewell!'

'Where's the boat?' Joshua asks – but the Seer is gone!

Josh shades his eyes as he looks around the dazzling-white beach. By a fringe of trees he spots a narrow track. Unable to bear standing around in the heat, he sets off to investigate the track, where lizards bake, comatosed by the broiling sun. As his shadow falls across the path the lizards skitter in all directions. He deftly sidesteps their erratic movements and looks from left to right … which way to the harbour? As he dithers uncertainly a seagull squawks over-head.

'AWWK!'

He immediately recognises the bird – it's the one who's been following him around at home.

'Hey, Mate! How have you followed me into the past?'

The bird cocks his head and flies up, then hovers, clearly waiting for Josh to follow him.

'Are you my guide?'

'AWWWK!' goes the bird.

'Tiresias said my journey starts here, so lead on!'

Mate turns on the wing and leads the bemused boy along the twisting track to the ancient port of Zachynthus.

Sailing boats of all shapes and sizes, with single eyes painted on both sides of their prows, jostle for space in the cramped harbour mouth where sailors wearing only loin cloths swab decks, grease oars and repair masts. On land they barter for fresh food. The noise is *deafening* but none of it is the familiar sound of the twenty-first century. There are no cars, no planes, no trains – no engines. The sound of the sea on the shingle beach, the boats rocking at anchor and the comings and going of the sailors combine to create a cacophony that Joshua finds quite overwhelming.

Concentrating hard, he gazes at the boats … how can he tell which of these ships is going to Elis? How much will a passage cost? Then he remembers he hasn't got any money. He may be in Ancient Greece but he reckons it still costs a few drachmas to bum a ride!

Suddenly a whiff of something so delicious hits his nostrils that he just has to follow it. Like a hungry dog he sniffs his way to a makeshift barbecue where a toothless old woman smacks her gums together as she turns spicy sausages on a red-hot grill. A boy about Joshua's age hands her a coin and in return she gives him two sausages in hot barley bread. The boy sinks his teeth into the sausage then spots Josh salivating beside him.

'Here,' he says in Ancient Greek that somehow Joshua has no problem understanding. 'Eat.'

The boy thrusts the food into his hands and Josh gobbles half the bread before he remembers his manners.

'Thank you,' he gulps. 'I'm Joshua Cross.'

'I'm Stavros – Stav. I'm going to Olympia.'

Joshua's impressed. 'Don't you have to go to school?' he asks.

Stav laughs. 'School! That's for the sons of rich lords and merchants. My father is a farmer. I've never been to school.'

'Can you read?'

'No, but I can run as fast as the wind and wrestle any boy my age. I'm going to Olympia to compete in the Olympic Games – why don't you come with me!'

Josh smiles at the athletic, olive-skinned boy with black hair and intense brown eyes. He might be in Ancient Greece but he's made a friend!

CHAPTER FOUR

Heracles

Stav knows where all the boats are going.

'Crete, Macedonia, Thrace, Thessaly, Corfu, Sicily – take your pick!' he says as they stand on the quay.

'Any for Elis?'

Stav points to a nearby boat with a red sail.

'That one, the *Dolphin*. She'll be sailing for Elis when the wind shifts.'

'How do we get a ride?'

'Jump ship.'

'You mean, *not pay*?'

Stav winks.

'I've just spent all my money on sausages!'

'So how do we get aboard?'

'Like this …'

Stav pulls him behind a row of barrels. He wets one of his index fingers and holds it up above his head as if it were an aerial.

'There's a good breeze gathering,' he announces. 'The *Dolphin* will sail soon.'

Josh's mouth is dry with fear. He wonders if they decapitate people who jump ship in Ancient Greece?

Stav hunkers down and peeps through a narrow gap in between two barrels. 'All clear!' he mutters and leaps aboard the *Dolphin*.

Josh cannot move. He is rooted to the spot with terror.

'Pssst! *Move it!*' hisses Stav.

Holding his breath Joshua waits for a couple of burly sailors to walk by before throwing himself over the side of the boat, rolling across the deck and dropping down into the hold.

'Over here!' whispers Stavros in the gloom.

Joshua hurries over and crouches down beside him. Shafts of sunlight filter through the metal grilles of the hold and he sees that the floor is swarming with cockroaches. 'UGH!' he groans as he feels them crunch under his feet.

'Better get used to them,' says Stavros. 'Along with the rats they're our fellow travellers to Elis.'

To illustrate his point Stavros takes a fig from a nearby crate and whizzes it into a dark corner. There's a sharp squeak then the biggest rat Josh has ever seen emerges from the shadows and slithers into one of the many crates in the hold.

Squashed between fruit crates, fat rats and wriggling cockroaches, they wait in the hold for the ship to set sail. Josh sighs with relief when he hears the sailors casting off. The ship shudders as the ropes are released and she slowly moves off. Seagulls screech as the *Dolphin*'s sail catches the breeze and she tacks out into the open sea.

'We're on our way!' says Stav excitedly.

'How long will it take?'

'About four hours.'

'*FOUR HOURS*!' They'll be knee-deep in rats and cockroaches by the time they dock! Josh gazes longingly at the sunlight shafting through the grilles. Suddenly a big seagull lands on top of the grille and cocks its head to one side.

'Hey, Mate! I'm here,' Joshua whispers.

'Why are you talking to a *bird*?' giggles Stav.

'He's my guide,' says Josh fondly. The bird gazes at him with his large yellow eyes then squawks indignantly as one of the crew passes by and kicks him. As the seagull flies up into the arching blue sky, Josh murmurs, 'Stay close!'

The heat in the hold is thick and oppressive. Stavros lies down and dozes off, but Josh is terrified of waking up with a cockroach in his mouth so he nods off standing up. He wakes to something dripping on to his head. Thinking it's water he wipes it away with the back of his hand, but when he looks he sees that his hands are stained a sticky red. He stares up and another drop lands on his face. Suddenly he realises that the sticky red stuff is *blood*! Overcome with horror he screams at the top of his voice.

'AHHHH!'

Stav jumps to his feet as the grille over the hold is swung open.

'Cheers, Josh. They'll cut our throats from ear to ear!'

Dragging the stowaways by the hair, the captain displays them to the crew and passengers.

'Shall I throw 'em overboard or hang 'em right before your eyes?'

For a split second Josh thinks he's joking. Nobody would treat kids like this, not even in Ancient Greece.

'Is he serious?' he whispers to Stav, who nods grimly.

'We'll die.'

Suddenly a voice calls out.

'Let the boys live – I'll pay their passage.'

All eyes swivel towards a man who is a giant! Immensely tall and immensely wide with shoulders like an ox, he stands before them wearing a lion-skin mini-toga! He has hands the size of frying pans and the biggest feet Josh has ever seen. The worked-out muscles on his body ripple as if they're in constant use. A mass of long blond hair hangs down to his shoulders like a lion's mane, but his face is child-like in its innocence. His eyes are clear and his smile is almost shy. He strides towards the captain and offers him two gold coins.

'Is that enough?'

The captain bites the coins. From the glint in his eye it's clearly *more* than enough. He grunts and pushes the boys towards the giant, who ushers them to the back of the boat.

'Oh, thank you, *thank you*!' cries Josh. 'It was *all* my fault. I screamed because blood was dripping on my head.'

Giant man smiles and lifts up a sack which is dripping blood through the planks of the deck.

'No, boy – it was MY fault.'

Seeing Josh go pale, Stav quickly slams one of his hands over his mouth.

'*Don't* scream again!' he whispers fiercely.

Deeply ashamed of his squeamishness, Josh nods. Agog with curiosity, Stav asks, 'So what's in the sack?'

Josh *seriously* doesn't want to know, but giant man seems keen to share his sack of blood with them.

'Have you heard of the Lion of Nemea?'

Both boys nod their head.

'It's a monstrous huge lion that nobody dares go near in case it rips their head off,' says Stav.

Giant man smiles and lifts a bloody dripping thing from the sack which he proudly holds up for their inspection. 'I ripped its head off!'

Mesmerised, Joshua gazes into the wide-open, amber eyes of the dead lion. Its purple-pink tongue lolls sideways out of its gaping mouth where shreds of flesh are visibly decomposing around the huge fangs.

'COOL!' raves Stavros.

To Joshua's immense relief, giant man carefully replaces the Nemean Lion's head back into the bloody sack.

'So how come you gave him the chop?' Stavros asks, keen to hear the gory details.

'It's a long story.'

'Hey, we've got time. We'll be in this tub all day.'

Giant man turns to Joshua, whose colour is now returning.

'Do you want to hear a hero's story?'

Joshua nods politely but wonders what horrors are about to unfold before him.

CHAPTER FIVE

The Lion of Nemea

'I am Heracles, son of Zeus.'

Enlightened by his blast of Ancient Greek knowledge, Joshua leaps to his feet with his eyes almost bugging out of his head.

'*HERACLES*! You're a HERO!'

Heracles drags him down. 'Shshsh!' he hisses as he holds him in a vice-like grip. 'I don't want everybody on board to hear who I am.'

'You're a legend, a hero – a superhero!' Joshua jibbers.

Slightly embarrassed by these praises, Heracles continues.

'My father is the great god Zeus but my mother is a mortal woman.'

Joshua interrupts excitedly. 'My friend Dido said that Zeus often fell in love with mortal women.'

'Your friend's right, but did she tell you that it causes huge problems with Hera his wife?'

Josh shakes his head. 'No. She never mentioned that.'

'When Hera heard of my birth she put serpents into my cradle to strangle me. I would have died if Zeus hadn't endowed me with strength as my birthright. I strangled the serpents in my chubby baby hands, but Hera vowed I would not live. She has tried to kill me many, many times … one day she will succeed.' He looks at the boys' shocked faces and quickly adds, 'There is one good thing. Athene, Goddess of Wisdom and Zeus's favourite child, protects me. She is like an angel at my side. It was she who sent me to speak with the Oracle at Delphi.'

'*You* went to speak with Apollo the Sun God?' gasps Stav.

Heracles nods.

'Apollo told me to do "Good Things" and help the world with my strength.'

'Good things? You mean your *labours*?' asks Joshua. 'I know seven of them,' he adds as he quickly reels them off. 'One, killing and skinning the Nemean Lion; two, slaughtering Hydra, the nine-headed monster; three, cleaning out the stables of King Augeas; four, capturing the fire-breathing Cretan bull; five, freeing the flesh-eating mares of Diomedes; six, picking the golden apples of the Hesperides; and seven, capturing Cerberus, the triple-headed hound who guards the gates of the Underworld.'

Heracles smiles modestly.

'Actually I've done twelve labours, but most people only remember seven. Anyway, back to Apollo the Sun God. He sent me off to be a servant in the court of King Eurystheus in Mycenae. The last thing Eurystheus wanted was a giant like me lumbering about the place, so he dreamt up difficult tasks for me to do, as far away from him as possible.'

The boys bend close as Heracles drops his voice to a whisper.

'Eurystheus always hoped that I'd get killed whilst I was away, but I'm like a bad drachma – I keep on turning up!'

'So what's the worst labour you've done?' asks Stav eagerly.

Heracles thinks hard. 'Almost certainly cleaning out the stables of the Augean horses.'

Stav looks disappointed. 'What's the big deal about cleaning out a stable? I do that all the time on my dad's farm.'

Heracles grins. 'A thousand horses lived in this stable which had never *ever* been cleaned out. The dung was two metres high! The air stank, the people stank, the horses stank – and I had to clean it out in *one day*!'

'So how did you do it?' asks Josh.

'First I moved the horses out, then I blocked two rivers with boulders the size of carts and redirected the rivers' flow straight through the stables.'

'*W-H-A-T?*' both boys gasp.

'The water roared down the mountainside and hit the stables with such force that it whooshed through all the filth and carried it out to sea,' he chuckles. 'It was quicker than mucking out for ten years!'

'Amazing!' splutters Stav.

'Where are you going now?' asks Josh.

'I should go back to King Eurystheus, but I'm heartily sick of being bossed about by him.'

Stavros is on his feet, electrified with excitement.

'Heracles, come to Olympia and show us how to win the Olympic Games!'

Heracles looks at the boys' excited faces. 'You know,' he says with a slow smile, 'I think I might do that!'

While Stavros is off buying food from the crew, Heracles turns to Josh and says, 'You speak our tongue and know our history, yet your skin is fair and your hair as pale as the moon. Where is your country?'

Joshua wriggles uncomfortably. He can't say he's from England, nobody would have heard of it – yet! Neither can he say he's from the future! Nobody would believe him.

'I live beyond Macedonia and Byzantium.'

Heracles smiles at his vagueness, as if he knows he's prevaricating.

'Is your land beyond the north wind?'

'Er, where does the north wind come from?'

Heracles laughs. 'The north of course!'

Josh nods his head. 'I live on an island in the far north.'

'Hyperborea,' Heracles says knowingly.

'You know it?' Josh asks in surprise.

Heracles nods. 'I have been there. It is drenched in rain cloud and the sun appears only once a year.'

'I wouldn't go that far! We have pretty good summers, though it does rain,' Josh admits.

'Would you like to tell me why you have travelled so far,

little Hyperborean?'

Joshua stares into Heracles' dark, brooding eyes. 'Can I trust you?'

In answer the giant man takes his hand and grips it firmly. 'You can trust me with your life.'

'I'm hiding from a man called Leirtod who's trying to kill me,' Josh blurts out. 'The blind seer called Tiresias who I met on the island of Zachynthus said I had to go on a journey, a hazardous journey, to meet my father. He said people would help me on my way.'

Heracles gives him a playful punch. 'Haven't you noticed, Joshua? People *are* helping you!'

Before they dock at Elis, Stav points out that the Lion of Nemea's head is beginning to pong. 'Shouldn't we dump your souvenir?' he asks.

'He was a fine lion,' says Heracles as he reluctantly drops the bloody sack overboard.

'Tell us how you killed him,' asks Stavros eagerly.

'With difficulty!' Heracles chuckles. 'He was as big as a horse, with a flaming mane and eyes that blazed fire. I hurled my spear at him, but instead of cutting into the lion's flesh the metal arrowhead shattered on impact.'

The boys stare at him, their eyes as big as saucers.

'So I grabbed my sword from my scabbard and tried to thrust it deep into the lion's chest, but the sword split clean in two.'

'Hahh!' gasp the spell-bound boys.

'Then I took my club and whacked it into the lion's open mouth. A blow like that should have killed him, but he just shook his head and ambled off.'

'*Then* what did you do?' gasps Stavros.

'I prayed to the goddess Athene – she protects me.'

'Smart move!' says Stav.

'She told me I had to use wisdom. So I decided to come at the Lion of Nemea *from behind*.'

'You mean you stabbed him up the bum!' laughs Josh.

'That would *not* have been a wise move!' says Heracles. 'I covered the lion's cave with a net and went in the *back* way. I caught him napping and grabbed him by the throat and squeezed the life out of him.'

'You strangled him with your *bare hands*?' gasps Joshua.

Heracles nods. 'Then I had to get the skin off his back.'

'Why?' asks Stavros.

'To prove that I'd killed him,' Heracles replies. 'But I couldn't find a weapon sharp enough to cut through his skin. Athene told me to cut off one of the lion's claws and use that. It went through his hide like butter!'

Keen on gory details, Stav asks, 'What did you do with the skin?'

Heracles smiles. 'I'm wearing it!'

CHAPTER SIX

Legends

When the *Dolphin* drops anchor in Elis harbour, Heracles strides down the gangplank with the boys proudly walking beside him.

'Do you know the way to Olympia?' Stav asks.

'Do *I* know the way?' laughs Heracles. 'I gave to the nation the land on which the Games take place!'

The boys gape at him.

'Remember I told you about those stinking stables that belonged to King Augeas?'

The boys nod.

'As a reward for cleaning out twenty years of manure he gave me a fine stretch of land, which I gave to the people so that they could hold their Games in honour of my father, Zeus.'

Heracles leads the boys out of the city of Elis into the rich countryside beyond, where the hot air throbs with the buzz of a thousand cicadas. Suddenly, over the clamour of the insects, they hear the sound of music. From a grove of olive trees a procession bursts out.

'We're going to Olympia!' somebody shouts. 'Join us!'

The procession is led by trumpeters. At least the noise they're making sounds like a trumpet but the instruments look more like a saxophone with a hat on! Behind the trumpeters are drummers, beating gourds of all shapes and sizes. Then come the crashing cymbal players.

The wild cacophony is softened by a high-pitched thrum from a stringed instrument which Joshua thinks must be the forerunner of the guitar. Behind the musicians come tumblers and acrobats who spring, cartwheel and leapfrog along the track. The boys join in the acrobatics but it's hard work doing cartwheels when the temperature's almost thirty-five degrees centigrade.

'I really need to get fit and start working out before the Games start,' says Stavros as he fails to keep up with a sprinting athlete twice his size.

'You're only a boy, you can't enter the Games,' says Josh.

'I can enter the *Boys'* Games,' Stav replies.

'Don't be daft! They don't have Boys' Games in the Olympics!'

'They *do!*'

'No they don't. It's only for men and women.'

Stav bursts out laughing. '*Women* aren't even allowed to watch the Games, never mind enter them!'

'My friend Dido would start a revolution if you told her she wasn't as good as a man,' Josh tells him.

Stav looks at him and shakes his head.

'Man, oh man, *where* are you coming from?'

As the evening stars prick the night sky, the procession stops by a winding river fringed with sweet-smelling pines. They pitch camp for the night on warm earth carpeted with wonderful wild flowers. As Joshua bends to examine them, Stav's tummy rumbles noisily.

'Great balls of fire! I'm starving,' groans Stav.

Josh's stomach rumbles too. It seems like a lifetime ago since they shared a sausage in Zachynthus harbour. Heracles volunteers to go and search for food and returns about an hour later with roasted meat and hot barley bread.

'Where did that come from?' asks Josh.

'Remember the goats at the back of the procession?' says Heracles. 'Tomorrow you'll find there are five fewer!'

'You mean we're eating those little goats?' splutters Josh.

'Of course! They're not going to Olympia for the relay race!' laughs Stav.

'Who killed them?'

'Me!' Heracles replied. 'I volunteered to slit their throats and butcher the carcasses in exchange for our supper.'

Joshua's twenty-first-century squeamishness disappears as he bites into the delicious roasted flesh of the tender young goats. Feeling full and satisfied, the boys settle down for the night. Stav instantly dozes off, but Josh sits close to Heracles, who is staring up at the starry sky.

'What are you thinking of?' he asks.

'My father, Zeus.'

'Do you ever see him?'

Heracles shakes his head. 'Hera forbids it.'

'It's lousy not being able to see your dad,' says Joshua sympathetically. 'I've seen pictures of Zeus in my history book at school – he looks *dead scary*!'

'He can be very fierce.'

'Why is Zeus always throwing thunderbolts across the sky?' Josh asks.

'He does that when he's in a bad temper,' Heracles explains. 'He's the God of Gods, Ruler of the Skies, and all Immortals should bow to his command. But his brothers and sisters are always arguing with him and that makes him very angry – hence the thunderbolts.'

'You'd think the Gods would all be happy up there on Mount Olympus, but they always seem to be arguing!' laughs Josh.

'Poseidon and Hades constantly bicker about who's the most powerful after Zeus. They both do sneaky things when they think the other one isn't looking.'

'Like stealing Persephone and taking her down into Hades,' says Joshua.

Heracles is impressed. 'Where did you learn that?'

'It's a mystery to me,' Joshua confesses. 'I think my father gave me knowledge of his world as I dreamt. I've never read anything at school but I suddenly know everything!'

'So you are the son of a lord in the far north?' asks Heracles.

'No. My family aren't rich.'

'Only the sons of wealthy lords and merchants go to school,' says Heracles.

'ALL children over the age of five go to school in my country. It's the law.'

'Why? Children should work. Education is wasted on poor boys.'

'Girls go to school too,' Josh adds.

Heracles looks genuinely shocked. 'Girls are fit for nothing but work and bearing children.'

It's Joshua's turn to be shocked. 'That's sexist!' he exclaims. 'Girls are as important as boys in my country. In fact my best friend is a girl and she's *brilliant*.'

'Are you betrothed to her?'

Joshua blushes at the thought. 'No, she's my friend!' he says quickly, then adds with a shy smile, 'But she does have lovely blue eyes!'

'A girl with blue eyes would be a rarity in Greece. She'd fetch a high price. You could sell her and buy a cow!'

Joshua bursts out laughing. If Dido heard Heracles say that she could be exchanged for a cow, she'd punch his lights out!

'Dido's really clever,' he says. 'Much cleverer than any boy I know.'

'It is better for girls to be ignorant and do as they're told.'

Josh bursts out laughing. 'It's a good thing Dido doesn't live in Ancient Greece – she never does as she's told!'

'In this country a disobedient girl would be thrown out

of her family home and left to die on the mountainside,' Heracles tells him grimly.

Josh decides it's time to change the subject.

'So what happened on Mount Olympus when Zeus found out about Hades taking Persephone into the Underworld.'

'Thunder roared and thunderbolts flashed! You see, Persephone is the only child of Demeter, Zeus's powerful sister and Goddess of the Harvest. In her anger she blasted the earth and ruined the harvest. When it looked like the whole of mankind would die of starvation, Zeus sent his son Hermes with a message for Hades. Zeus demanded that Persephone should be released immediately, on condition that no food had passed her lips during her stay in the Underworld.'

'Why couldn't she eat down there?' Josh asks curiously.

'Because anyone who has eaten the food of the dead owes allegiance to Hades, their king,' Heracles explains. 'Persephone said she had eaten nothing since she had been dragged from her home. So Hermes took Persephone back to the entrance of the Underworld where Cerberus, the hound who guards the gates, licked her hand in farewell. She was returned to her mother and the cold winter fell away! The fields turned green, and spring corn sprouted among the fragrant wild flowers. Demeter's joy was bound-less and was reflected in the beautiful blossom that bloomed in every treetop.

'But her happiness was short lived. Down in the

Underworld, Hades discovered that Persephone had swallowed seven tiny pomegranate pips.

'"Persephone must be returned to me," he told Zeus. "She has eaten the food of the dead and she belongs to me."

'Demeter refused point blank to part with her daughter, so an urgent discussion was held among the gods. They decided that for nine months of the year Persephone would live with her mother on earth, but for the remaining three she had to return to Hades and rule as queen of the Underworld. Every year Demeter mourns the loss of her daughter. The flowers shrivel, the birds cease to sing and the trees shed their leaves. But every year on Persephone's return, spring comes back again and Demeter, Goddess of the Harvest, blesses the earth in abundance.'

'Pity about those pomegranate seeds,' yawns Josh as he stretches out on the warm ground and gazes up at the myriad stars twinkling overhead.

Heracles smiles as he settles down beside Joshua.

'Sleep well, Hyperborean,' he whispers. 'May all the gods protect you.'

CHAPTER SEVEN

Olympia

They wake early next morning and Josh reaches for his dirty old jeans.

'You can't put those rags on,' says Stavros.

'Why not? They're my clothes.'

'You look like a slave,' says Stav. 'You should wear one of these, like me.'

Joshua looks at the white garment in his hands.

'It looks like a sheet,' he remarks.

'It's called a *chiton*.'

'They nearly sound the same.'

'Come on, hold up your arms and let me put it on you.'

Joshua lifts his arms and Stav pins the folded cloth at the shoulders then ties a belt around it.

'Now you look like a Greek,' he says.

Josh looks at the short hem fluttering above his bony white kneecaps.

'I am NOT wearing a skirt!'

'It's a tunic. It's very cool in the heat – we all wear them.'

'It might be cool in the heat, but it's very uncool for a

boy to walk around in a skirt.'

'What do men in your country wear?' asks Stav.

'Trousers like these,' says Josh holding up his old jeans. 'They keep your legs warm when it's cold.'

'That's all right for Hyperborea but it's not cold here,' Stav points out.

Josh can't argue with that. The sun which has only recently risen is already frying him. He remembers the coin in his jeans' pocket and the little purse of white barley which Tiresias gave to him on the island of Zachynthus.

'Where do I keep things like money?' he asks.

Stav takes a drachma and shoves it in his mouth. 'We carry our money tucked inside our cheeks,' he mumbles.

Josh bursts out laughing. 'You're kidding!'

Stav removes the money from his mouth. 'If you want to look after your money, your mouth is a very safe place.'

Josh shakes his head in disbelief. 'What happens if you swallow it?'

Stav grins and shrugs his shoulders. 'You wait until the next day then you find it.'

'YUK!'

Their small procession sets off early and Joshua is glad of his cool, short chiton which is much more comfortable than his hot jeans. He puts the coin to pay Charon the Ferryman into the purse with the white barley and holds on to it very tightly. Not convinced that Stav was telling him the truth, he asks Heracles where he keeps his money. Heracles opens his mouth and takes out several small coins.

'In my cheeks – where else?'

Their conversation is halted by the arrival of a much bigger procession than their own small one. Athletes, horses, trainers, charioteers, souvenir sellers, merchants on donkeys, and dozens of women and children carrying baskets of doves, or leading oxen, donkeys, rams and goats, trudge along beside them. Josh anxiously eyes the animals.

'Are they supper?' he asks.

'No, they're the animals that will be used for sacrificial slaughter,' Stav explains.

'ALL of them?'

Stavros nods. 'And *hundreds* more besides. The gods have to be satisfied, otherwise the Games will go badly.'

They're now surrounded by hundreds of people and the babble of their different voices is tumultuous.

'Where are they all from?' Joshua asks intrigued.

'Crete, Thrace, Ionia, Thesprotis, the Cyclades, Aetolia …' Stav laughs. '*Everywhere*! This is BIG entertainment!'

'We're now on the Sacred Way and have joined up with travellers who have walked thirty-six miles along the coastline. They'll have stopped off at every temple and shrine en route to sacrifice to the gods and pray for success in the—'

Heracles stops as a nearby souvenir seller bellows at the top of his voice.

'Get out of it!'

His roar is followed by a high-pitched scream of pain, and a tiny puppy scuttles out from under his kicking feet.

Unfortunately, in her haste to escape the pup dashes straight into the path of a fat merchant on a donkey, which almost treads on her. The merchant irritably whacks the pup with his horse whip, sending her flying into a heap of steaming horse muck in the middle of the road. The crowd laugh and point at the filthy pup who whines pathetically as she lifts her head out of the filth.

'Poor thing!' exclaims Joshua. 'We can't leave it there.'

'We can – it stinks!' exclaims Stav. 'Forget the runt – it'll be dead in an hour!'

'No way!'

Joshua hurries over to the pile of horse muck and lifts the puppy out of it. Trying to ignore the smell, he strokes her silky little ears. Stav wrinkles his nose in disgust.

'Ugh, it's covered in *muck*!'

Josh smiles as he tucks the pup into a fold of his chiton.

'I don't mind a bit of muck!'

As soon as they get to Olympia, Stav switches gear. In a blink of an eye the street-wise Greek kid transforms into a *serious athlete* in training.

'I'm hitting that gymnasium and working up a sweat,' he announces. 'Coming?'

Josh nods; he's keen to see his friend working out. Stavros points to the little bundle tucked underneath Josh's shirt.

'Don't bring that stinking dog!'

'Nobody will see her.'

'But they'll SMELL her!'

'That's OK – just say it's *me*!' laughs Josh.

Heracles takes the pup and dumps her unceremoniously into the nearest water trough. She wriggles in protest but comes out smelling a lot sweeter.

'Now she looks like a sewer rat!' laughs Stav as Josh dries her brown coat, which is sticking to her skeletal-thin ribs.

Josh pops Muck back into the nice baggy fold of his chiton and they set off for the gymnasium, which is a huge space – much, much bigger than any gym Josh has ever seen in the twenty-first century. Naked athletes are everywhere – lifting weights, limbering up, running around the track and practising their take-off from the starting blocks.

'OK, strip!' says Heracles.

Stav has his kit off in a flash; Josh can only gape in total disbelief.

'I'm a *spectator*.'

'No you're not – you're a contestant,' snaps Heracles. 'STRIP!'

'But I'm used to running with clothes ON!'

'Then get used to running with them OFF!' laughs Stav as he sets off jogging around the gymnasium.

'What about Muck?' worries Josh.

Heracles raises his shaggy eyebrows. 'I'll look after the pup on condition that you get your clothes off and start exercising.'

Josh sticks the pup under Heracles' lion-skin tunic. 'DEAL!'

By the time Josh strips off his clothes, Stavros is building up a heavy sweat working out with the weights. Josh joins him. He grabs one of the weights which he tries to lift – the next thing he knows, he's flat on his face on the marble floor!

'Aaaa … they're heavy!'

'Do it like this,' says Stav. He gives the weight an expert flip and slowly stretches his arms up until he's holding it over his head.

Josh tries again but can't even get it off the ground! Seeing him struggle, Heracles puts the sleeping pup down in a corner and comes to his aid. In awesome silence Joshua watches him lift the weights like they are a bunch of grapes.

'Which part of my body am I working the hardest?' asks Heracles as he stands firm as an oak tree.

Joshua carefully studies his body, which is a mass of rippling muscles.

'Your arms?' he guesses.

'No! Look at my feet, see how they're placed …'

Josh stares at Heracles' huge plates of meat firmly planted on the marble floor. His calf muscles are bulging, his knees are tense, his thighs and buttocks are clenched, but his breathing is nice and easy as he holds the weights over his head.

'My whole body is carrying the load,' says Heracles. 'Come on – give it a go.'

'I'm such a wimp!' moans Josh.

'Everybody starts somewhere,' says Heracles. 'You start here!'

After an arduous workout in the gymnasium, Heracles takes the boys to the bathhouse.

'Wow! A swimming pool,' cries Josh excitedly. 'I'm good at the front crawl. Hey, I could enter a *swimming* race!'

'There aren't any swimming races in the Olympic Games,' Stav tells him.

'No swimming?'

'We have foot races, discuss, javelin, wrestling, boxing, pentathlon, long jump, horse racing, chariot racing – but *no* swimming.'

Josh grins. 'Shame. Bang goes my chance of a gold medal!'

'Athletes don't win medals,' Stav tells him. 'They're crowned with wreaths made from olive leaves picked from sacred groves.'

Josh winks. 'I don't think any of those sacred olive wreaths have got my name on them!'

The bathhouse is brilliant. It even has a sauna, heated from under-floor piping. Joshua is surprised when a slave boy approaches Heracles and starts to scrape his back with a small wooden instrument that looks like a little scythe.

'What's he doing?' he asks Stav.

'Before we exercise we rub oil into our skin to make it

supple. The steam in here lifts the oil and the dirt from our pores and the slave scrapes it off with a strigil.'

Fascinated, Josh watches the child, who can be no more than six years old, wipe oily scum off his strigil.

'Poor kid, I wouldn't like his job!'

Stavros shrugs. 'Slaves are like dogs. They do as they're told – or die!'

Joshua wants to disagree with him, but after a gruelling workout followed by a warm bath, he's feeling so relaxed his eyes keep drooping – then he remembers that he's left his dog in the gymnasium.

'MUCK!' he cries, startling everybody. 'I've left her in the gym!'

He runs naked through the hot streets and gets to the gym just in time to find one of the coaches booting Muck out of the door.

'No vermin allowed!' he snarls as Joshua grabs the pup. 'If I see that mutt in here again I'll wring its neck.'

Josh cuddles her and she gives him a big wet lick on the nose.

'It's tough being a pup in Ancient Greece!'

Stav and Heracles are waiting for him outside the bath-house.

'If you insist on keeping that dog, we'd better get a bag to put her in,' says Heracles.

'Yeah, I don't want to spend the entire Olympic Games

running around after a stinking puppy – talk about a bad press!' grumbles Stav.

In the marketplace Heracles buys grapes, goat's milk, curd cheese, honey still in its honeycomb, fresh bread and a soft leather bag which he hands to Josh.

'Put Muck in there – at least we'll know where she is!'

Before Muck's introduced to her new mobile home, Josh feeds her bread dipped in milk, which she wolfs down. When she's full up and contented, he tucks her into the leather pouch, along with the precious gifts Tiresias gave him, then secures it tightly around his waist.

'Better not try a bout of wrestling with that wrapped around you,' jokes Stav. 'You could end up with one flat pooch!'

To avoid the scorching heat of the day, they sit in the shade of the Palaestra, a large square building with a court-yard in the middle where wrestlers practise. Joshua's eyelids droop. He feels a bit like Muck, full up and sleepy, but Heracles (being a legend) has no such human frailties.

'Boxing and wrestling next!' he announces.

Josh yawns. 'How about a break?'

Heracles shakes his head. 'The Boys' Games are *tomorrow* – you must practise *today*.'

Thanks to his brother, Joshua's spent half his formative years dodging punches and kicks. Fights in the playground perfected his basic skills to an art form. His brilliance at headlocks is surpassed by none at school. Even Heracles is impressed by his ability to get out of an armlock.

'Where did you learn that trick?' he enquires.

'At home!'

Stav's intrigued. 'Do you live in a gymnasium?'

'No, I live in a chip shop.'

'What's chop ship?' asks Stav, getting it wrong.

'*CHIP SHOP*,' Josh corrects him. 'It's as hot and greasy as a gymnasium but we sell food—'

Heracles and Stav look puzzled.

'Chips, potatoes, meat pies, gravy, peas – mega-lard?' Josh elaborates, but he can see that his friends are none the wiser. 'Forget it – let's box!'

Heracles takes the boys into one of the training rooms off the Palaestra, where he wraps bands of soft leather around their fists.

'Slaps with the open hand, punches with the fists and blows with the back of the hand are allowed. Kicking is also permitted, but no headbutting.'

'Phew, what a relief – headbutting was never my speciality!' jokes Josh.

'The fight goes on without a break until one of you has had enough,' continues Heracles.

'How do you know when we've had enough?' asks Josh.

'You raise your right hand in the air,' Heracles explains.

Josh turns to Stav. 'Listen mate, if I raise my right arm in the air take that as a submission and don't snap it off!'

'OK, box!' yells Heracles.

Stavros comes charging at Josh who flicks a fist at him. Stavros lumbers around swinging punches but he can't get close to Josh, whose footwork is swift and nifty.

'You're tougher than I thought,' mutters Stav as he struggles in a leg-lock which finally brings him down. Heracles teaches them a couple of clever throwing moves, then he shows them how to twist out of various body locks.

'You'll do well,' he says at the end of the session, which leaves both boys dripping with sweat. 'Why don't you take a bathe in the river while I try and find some supper?'

The boys tear down to the River Alpheus and throw themselves into the cool clear water. Muck whines pathetically from the riverbank, torn between wanting to be with her master and hating getting her paws wet! Stav dive-bombs Josh and makes a grab for his legs. Struggling and laughing the boys lunge and punch at each other until they can hardly stand.

'I've had it!' cries Stav as he throws himself on the river-bank.

'Me too,' gasps Josh as he flops down beside him.

When they get their breath back, they skim pebbles across the silky-smooth surface of the water, which reflects the gold and crimson of the slow-setting sun.

'What's your ambition?' Stav suddenly asks.

Josh is stunned by his question. Since he arrived in the past he's hardly given a thought to the future.

'To see my dad. What's yours?'

'To win every game in the Boys' Olympics and stay here *forever*.'

'But the Games are every *four years*! What will you do

when this one ends?'

'Stay on and work with the trainers until I'm the fastest sprinter in Greece. I could coach other athletes too and work in the bathhouse – I'd do *anything* to stay right here in this sacred place.'

Josh smiles at the blazing passion in his friend's intense brown eyes. 'If you believe in something as much as you do, Stav, it's bound to come true.'

'Where will you go after the Games?'

Josh can't bring himself to say, I'm heading for the Fields of Joy, just beyond Hades, to meet my dad! 'Oh, here and there,' he answers vaguely.

The awkward moment passes with the arrival of Heracles bearing roasted-kid kebabs, which Muck is *very* partial to! After their meal the boys lie back, tired and con-tented, and watch the first stars prick the night sky. Josh sighs heavily.

'I reckon I'm going to be lousy at the Games tomorrow.'

'Pray to the gods for their protection,' Stav advises.

'You've got so *many* gods – which one shall I pray to?'

'Pray to my father, Zeus – the Games are in his honour,' says Heracles.

Josh closes his eyes. 'Please Zeus, I pray that I won't look a wally tomorrow!'

'What's a *wally*?' Heracles asks.

'The opposite of a hero like you.'

'Heracles is the greatest hero!' says Stav admiringly.

'There are many legendary heroes in Ancient Greece,'

Heracles replies modestly. 'Some of the brightest constellations are named after them.'

'Tell me a legend,' Josh begs.

'See that constellation over there in the west … ?'

Josh follows Heracles' pointing finger.

'That's named after the hero Perseus. My father, Zeus, fell in love with a beautiful mortal woman called Danae, and nine months later Perseus was born. Danae's father, King Acrisius, had been told in a prophecy that if his daughter ever bore a son, it would kill him. He put baby Perseus and his mother into a wooden crate, which he threw into the sea where he hoped they'd both perish.

'Zeus stepped in and rescued them. He sent them to the island of Seriphos, where their wooden crate landed on a beach that belonged to a kind fisherman. He looked after the mother and baby, and when Perseus grew up he taught him to fish. Unfortunately the King of Seriphos spotted lovely Danae and wanted to marry her, but she refused him. The King decided that he might do a lot better with the mother if the son was out of the way so he sent for Perseus and played a trick on him.

'"There are a lot of nasty rumours flying around about you," he said.

'"What rumours?" Perseus demanded.

'"Oh, that you're a bit of a softie – a mummy's boy!"

Perseus was furious. 'I am *not* a mummy's boy!' he raged.

'"Of course you're not – that's exactly what I said," the

cunning King replied. "I suggest you do something really heroic so that people will stop doubting your bravery."

'Perseus promptly agreed. "What shall I do?"

'The King smiled. This was exactly how he hoped the boy would react.

'"Kill the Medusa!"

'Perseus went pale. The Medusa was the deadliest of all the Gorgon monsters with a hideous head entwined with writhing, hissing snakes. Anyone who looked at its face was instantly turned to stone.

'"If you were to kill the Medusa and bring back her head, nobody would ever call you a mummy's boy again," coaxed the wicked king.

'"Right, I'll do it," said Perseus and set off for the far north to find the Medusa. His father Zeus knew that his young son couldn't fight the monster single-handed, so he asked all the gods and goddesses on Mount Olympus to bless him with gifts. Hermes tied wings to his sandals so that he could fly like a bird. Hades gave him a helmet to protect him in battle. But it was wise Athene who gave him the greatest gift.'

Spellbound by the story Josh asks, 'What did she give him?'

'A shield.'

'A *shield* to fight off a monster with a hideous head entwined with writhing snakes! You must be joking.'

'Ah, but you don't know how he's going to use it.'

'There's only one way of using a shield,' reasons Joshua.

'Anyway, how's he going to kill the monster if he can't look at it?'

'This is where Athene's wisdom comes in. She told Perseus to look into the shield, which was polished like silver so it would reflect everything.'

'So he could see the Medusa reflected in the shield? Brilliant!' cries Josh.

'You just said the shield was useless,' teases Heracles.

'So I got it wrong. You Ancient Greeks are cleverer than me!' Joshua jokes. 'Go on.'

'Perseus set off for the far northern lands of the Hyperboreans – where you come from, boy. With wings on his sandals, Perseus was able to fly across the world like a swallow! When he reached the cave where the Medusa lived, he found it surrounded by dozens of stone statues.'

'Ah! Were they people who'd looked at the Medusa and been turned to stone?'

Heracles nods and continues his story.

'Holding his shield high, Perseus walked backwards into the monster's den and caught sight of the Medusa, reflected in his silver shield. She was HUGE! She scuttled towards him, a mountain of flesh, and instead of hair on her head she had snakes that writhed and hissed all over her face.

'Perseus held his ground until the beast was right behind him. When he could feel her stinking hot breath on his neck, he whirled around with his sword flashing. Keeping his eyes firmly shut, Perseus swiped the air around the Medusa and WHOOSH! – he chopped her head clean off. Even though her head was separated from her body the monster kept on shrieking … then suddenly everything went quiet. The monster was dead but still Perseus didn't look at it – Athene had warned him that even dead the Medusa could turn him to stone.

'With his eyes tight shut he picked up the head and shoved it into a sack, then he flew back to Seriphos as fast as he could. But things had gone badly for his mother in his absence. Perseus found Danae dressed in wedding clothes, weeping.

'"The king is forcing me to marry him," she sobbed.

'Seething with anger Perseus grabbed his sack and hurried to the king who was *very* surprised to see him.

'"I've got a wedding present here which you'll never forget," he said as he handed over the sack.

The king opened it and stared straight into the face of the decapitated Medusa. In seconds he was turned into a statue of stone.'

Josh jubilantly punches the air and disturbs Stavros, who dropped off to sleep halfway through the story.

'That's a great legend,' he says, then he remembers the beginning of the story. 'So did Perseus ever kill his grand-dad?'

'Of course, the gods' prophecies *always* come true.'

'How did it happen?'

'Perseus became a legendary discuss thrower in the Olympic Games. One year, in a place called Larissa where he was competing in the funeral games for a local king, he threw the discuss and accidentally struck and killed a spectator. It was Acrisius, his grandfather. Thus was the oracle fulfilled.'

Josh's excitement wakes up Muck who walks off to relieve herself by the river Alpheus. Josh follows her. As he stands staring up at the twinkling star-shape of Perseus winging his way across the night sky, a shadow crosses the moon and a voice like metal rasps in his ear.

'It didn't take long to find you, son of Lumaluce!'

Too terrified to move, Josh stands rooted to the spot. His mouth is dry, his tongue stuck to his palate.

'Your father thought he could hide you in history. Such foolishness. To think that after all this time I'd lose the joy of claiming you just because you'd disappeared out of the twenty-first century.'

Joshua's thoughts are racing around his head. His father's plan to hide him in the past has badly backfired. Leirtod has tracked him down in no time.

'I have looked forward to your disposal for many, many centuries. I won't be fobbed off with stupid tricks,' he whispers malevolently.

Joshua's stomach turns to water as Leirtod reaches into the folds of his cloak and brings out a jewelled blade that glimmers in the moonshine. His legs give way beneath him as he falls to the ground and lands on Muck, who yelps and scampers off.

'I've done nothing to harm you!' he cries.

'It is enough that you are the son of my enemy,' snarls Leirtod as the jewelled knife flashes in his hand.

Joshua closes his eyes and waits to die, but suddenly he hears a fluttering of wings followed by a furious squawk.

'AWWWK!'

The knife in Leirtod's hand falls to the ground as Mate boldly flaps in his face.

'You will not kill my son!' booms a voice that Josh instantly recognises. It's his father!

'He is mine!' rages Leirtod.

'Hatred has affected your brilliance, Leirtod. Your force over Joshua was stronger in the twenty-first century where you were only competing against mortals. By slipping time you have greatly reduced your power.'

'A few millennia cannot weaken me!'

'But it has. Your wit and your strength *are* reduced. Look, the blade lies at your feet. Here in Ancient Greece you are surrounded by the Immortals, who favour *me*. They will sap your power and your reasoning.'

Leirtod cries out in fury and lunges for the knife. His father's voice rings out.

'RUN JOSHUA!'

He springs to his feet but Leirtod grabs him in a vice-like grip. He suddenly remembers the leg-lock manoeuvre that Heracles taught him and Stav earlier that day in the gymnasium. He lunges forwards and yanks Leirtod's legs from underneath him.

'I'll kill you!' he screams in fury, but Josh is running for his life. He sprints like an antelope – and runs slap-bang into what at first he thinks is a tree. It is in fact Heracles who's been alerted by Muck and has come to his rescue. Heracles pushes Josh to one side and faces Leirtod, who stops dead in his tracks at the sight of the giant.

'Don't lay a hand on him,' says Heracles in a voice like granite.

Leirtod tries to snatch at Joshua but Heracles pushes him away.

'Go, evil one, before I rip your head off your shoulders.'

Leirtod's dark eyes glitter with malice. 'Hera will *burn* you!' he hisses and, swirling his cloak around his face, melts into the night.

Heracles takes Joshua back to camp where he is rapturously welcomed by Muck. As he settles down beside Stav, who is sleeping like a baby, Josh whispers, 'My father saved me – he *protects* me!' He adds joyfully, 'I've never seen him, apart from in my dreams, but I feel him all around me.'

Heracles smiles tenderly.

'I was scared to death but I felt so strong knowing that I was Lumaluce's son.'

'Lumaluce is one of our great legends.'

'You know him?' gasps Joshua.

'Everybody in the Ancient World knows of your father. He sent me to protect you.'

'He sent YOU to ME?'

'Yes, you needed protecting and I am the strongest mortal in Ancient Greece at this moment in time!' Heracles answers with a modest smile.

'Why didn't you tell me?'

'Because I wanted to watch you and find out if you had your father's spirit.'

Joshua gulps nervously. 'Have I?'

'Oh yes! You are his son.'

Joshua glows with pride. 'I can't wait to see my father.'

'You still have a difficult journey ahead of you,' Heracles tells him urgently. 'I have things to give you on your way.'

'Tiresias gave me a coin to pay Charon the Ferryman and a little bag of white barley that I haven't a clue what to do with.'

'Take great care of them, Joshua, they are essential to your entry into Hades.'

'What have you got for me, Heracles?'

'Advice.'

'What advice?'

'Advice on how to get into the Underworld where only the dead enter.'

Joshua's brow crinkles with anxiety. 'I'm scared of going there,' he admits.

'We'll talk of these things tomorrow. Sleep now, son of Lumaluce. You will need your strength for the Games.'

As Joshua snuggles down he remembers Leirtod's hateful words.

'Will Hera *really* burn you?'

Heracles strokes the hair back from his worried brow.

'Hera has vowed to kill me. You must know by now, Joshua – the gods will not be denied.'

'Aren't you afraid?'

Heracles shakes his head. 'I am weary, Joshua. I look forward to leaving this world and resting for all eternity.'

Tears sting Joshua's eyes.

'You're my friend. I don't want you to die.'

'Sleep little Hyperborean – tomorrow you run with the legends!'

CHAPTER EIGHT

The Games

The boy contestants gather at dawn and line up in the gymnasium under the beady eye of the chief coach, Theagenes. Josh's heart sinks all the way down his greased naked body into his bare feet. The boys beside him are strongly built and well worked out – they all look like baby Heracles in the making! There's only one other skinny kid and that's Milos from Rhodes. Josh wonders what games he'll do ... egg and spoon? Probably not the sort of game they'd appreciate in Ancient Greece. Not sweaty enough!

Theagenes goes down the line checking with each boy what games he's entered for. Stavros proudly announces, '*Everything*!' When it comes to Josh's turn he blushes and mutters, 'Er, maybe boxing.'

Heracles calls from the back of the gymnasium, '*Definitely* boxing!'

Theagenes salutes Heracles. 'I'll see to it, lord.'

Joshua smiles feebly and wishes he didn't have friends in such high places!

The boxing begins. Josh gets through two gruelling rounds then meets his final opponent, Nikos from Skios, who eyeballs him with hatred. The ref approaches and binds the boys' knuckles with soft leather bands.

'No gouging out eyeballs, headbutting or biting!' yells the ref, and they're off. Nikos comes at Josh like a charging bull elephant, knocking him flat! Josh hardly regains his breath before Nikos is pummelling into his back! Josh wants to fight back but he's dazed by the blows his opponent is raining down on him. Suddenly there's blood all over his face.

'Break!' yells the ref.

Josh slumps to the ground where Heracles gently sponges his split lip.

'What's wrong with you, boy?' he asks. 'Why don't you retaliate?'

'He's belting me so hard I can't think straight.'

'Look into his eyes and imagine the face of your enemy – imagine Leirtod. That should make you wild!'

Josh bounces back into the ring and as Nikos spins to hit him hard in the chest he does what Heracles advised. He imagines the stark-white face of Leirtod and his glittering, hate-filled eyes. His heart races and his hands itch to punch out. Gritting his teeth in fury, Josh darts forward and hits his opponent hard in the belly. As he gasps and bends over double, Josh punches him in the ribs. Nikos grunts and swings a couple of feeble punches but Josh is dancing around him. Then WHAM! Josh smacks Nikos from Skios hard under the chin and he's out for the count! Heracles runs in and crowns Joshua with a wreath of sacred olive leaves then lifts him high in the air.

'The Hyperborean boy is the *WINNER*!' he cries, his voice ringing out with pride.

Josh waves his arms in triumph. *Never* in his wildest dreams did he ever imagine winning in the Olympics! If only Stevie could be here to share this supreme moment of triumph.

Meanwhile Stav has won first place in the discuss throwing *and* the javelin events. They find him in the stadium completing the pentathlon event with the long jump. Josh is surprised to see a group of slaves playing their lyres to accompany the athletes as they make the long jump.

'Music helps them with their timing,' Heracles explains.

Josh points to the stone weights that Stav is swinging in his hands.

'What's he doing with those?'

'They build up a good rhythm before take off,' Heracles explains.

Taking deep breaths Stav swings the weights, then from a standing start he takes a mighty jump and clears a good six metres.

'WOW! That's got to be a record!' cries Joshua.

Heracles cautions him.

'Don't jump to conclusions – there are other contestants.'

When skinny Milos from Rhodes takes up his position, Joshua bursts out laughing.

'This guy's no competition!'

Milos swings the weights, looking like a weedy bird ready for flight. But when he takes off, Josh's laughter turns to awe. He seems to *fly* through the air before he lands on the seven-metre marker and breaks all the records. Theagenes the trainer stares at him, deeply impressed.

'You've got a serious future with the long jump, kid!'

At the end of the day the boys are utterly exhausted but *so* happy. Stavros is *loaded* with olive wreaths and has been asked by Theagenes to stay on and work in the gymnasium, assisting him with training athletes, in return for which he will be trained himself. It is Stavros's greatest dream come true. He can hardly contain his joy, which slowly becomes tinged with sadness as he realises that he and Josh have only another day left together. Heracles is subdued too. Only little Muck is light-hearted. She frisks around in the darkness, chasing after dry leaves and moonbeams.

The day with all its tests and triumphs catches up with Josh, who drops off into a deep sleep. He wakes up with a start to the sound of a loud screech.

'AWWWK!'

Josh looks up and sees his seagull friend perched in a tree directly overhead.

'MATE!'

The sight of the beady-eyed bird brings back a rush of memories: Shakespeare's Chippy, his mum's warm smile, Stevie and Dido teasing him about missing a vital goal, the

London Eye turning over the swift-flowing waters of the River Thames, the Union Jack fluttering high over the Houses of Parliament. A pang of homesickness shoots through him, immediately replaced by a pang of dismay as Mate squawks and flies off.

'No, don't go!'

Mate swerves on the wing and turns to Josh, who *knows* the seagull's telling him to follow. He leaves Stav sleeping beside Heracles and dashes after the bird, who leads him into a grove of olive trees. Josh is immediately shrouded in darkness. He can't see Mate but he hears him squawk close by. Tensing his body Josh moves deeper into the cloying darkness. Suddenly he hears an evil laugh followed by a familiar high-pitched yap. Muck! panics Josh. They've got my dog! Barefoot he slinks under the twisted olive boughs then stops and dives for cover as the moon drifts out from behind the clouds and lights up the olive grove. Crouching low he spies two shadowy figures. One is Leirtod – the other is the monstrous centaur.

'Hippodrax, do *exactly* as I say,' says Leirtod.

The beast squeals and rears up on its hind legs.

'Kill the dog and lay its head and entrails on the altar. The son of Lumaluce will mourn his pet but he will not grieve for long. Soon he will join it in the afterworld.'

The notion obviously amuses Leirtod who laughs loudly, a dry rasping laugh that holds no humour. Excited by his master's laughter, Hippodrax grunts then snatches up Muck in his arms and gallops out of the grove. Hearing his pup's tortured screams makes Josh long to run to her rescue but he forces himself to stay hidden. Whispering low he turns to Mate, who's perched close by on an olive bough.

'Follow them.'

Mate swoops up out of the shadows.

'AWWK!' he screeches as he flies out of the grove.

Startled by the noise Leirtod tenses and looks around. By the light of the moon Josh sees that the expression on his face is that of fear. Who is he frightened of?

'Who's there?' he calls. 'Is that you, Lumaluce?' he calls again.

The only sound to be heard is the breeze soughing through the treetops. Cursing under his breath Leirtod swirls his cloak around his face and melts into the darkness.

When he's gone Joshua runs out of the olive grove and sets off in pursuit of Muck. As he races up the steep hill-slope bathed in liquid moonlight, he realises he's learnt something vital tonight. Leirtod is *afraid* of his father!

He catches up with Mate hovering over Hippodrax, who is galloping up the precipitous pathways with Muck struggling in his grip. Josh breaks into a sprint but can't gain on Hippodrax, who skips and leaps over boulders and rock-faces. Mate hangs back to wait for him but Josh urges him on.

'Get Muck before the beast kills him!' he gasps.

Mate swoops high over the mountain where he hovers like a hawk. Suddenly he folds in his wings and drops like an arrow, with his sharp yellow beak aimed straight at

Hippodrax's backside. He hits the beast bang on target, making him squeal in pain. Hippodrax rears up and tries to swipe out at Mate but the bird is far too quick for him. He darts away then starts to circle down; round and round he goes. From his rocky perch Hippodrax watches, mesmerised. His demonic head follows the bird's slow descent … round and round and round. Suddenly the beast falls over, dazed with dizziness. Mate seizes the moment. He zooms in, and scooping up Muck by one of her little paws, he bears her up into the air. Hippodrax squeals and bucks in fury but Mate clears the mountain ridge and flies back to the safety of Olympia.

Joshua tears down the mountain slope, desperate to catch up with Mate – desperate to find out if Muck is alive. His heart almost stops in fear when he sees the bird by the river gently nudging a small bundle of fur. '*Please, please* don't let Muck be dead,' Josh prays to all the Immortal gods as he throws himself down on the ground. He gasps in relief as he feels the puppy breathing, then gently picks her up and cradles her in his hands.

'Shshh, you're all right now,' he whispers. 'I've got you …'

Suddenly Muck stirs, opens her eyes and feebly wags her little tail. Josh kisses her tenderly on the nose.

'You're safe!'

'AAAWK!' goes Mate and flies off.

'Thank you for saving her life!' Josh calls after him.

Mate turns on the wing and Josh swears he's winking at him!

CHAPTER NINE

Sacrifice

Joshua is shaken awake by Heracles. He blearily opens his eyes to a sun as red as a blood orange peeping over the eastern sky, promising yet another baking-hot day in Ancient Greece. Heracles gives him another shake.

'Get up or you'll miss the procession.'

Stav is full of beans and keen to get started but Muck and Josh, who have spent half the night being chased by demons, struggle to their feet and sleepily consume the bread and warm goat's milk that Heracles provides.

'Come on,' urges Stavros impatiently. 'That's the trumpet blasting – the procession's underway!'

Josh hasn't a clue what's going on but he tucks Muck into the pouch tied around his waist then runs after Stavros and Heracles, who have joined the cheering crowd of spectators lining the route to Olympia.

'May the goddess Nike bless your race!' they call out to the procession of bronzed, naked athletes who barely acknowledge their greetings – they look neither to left nor right but walk purposefully forwards, their thoughts concentrated only on success. Suddenly a huge cloud of dust appears, causing the crowd to cough and splutter. The dust grows denser and Josh hears a loud rhythmic tramping – a noise so loud it sounds like growling thunder. Through the gagging dust appear a thousand oxen, whipped on by slaves.

'Where are they going?' gasps Josh.

'They are to be sacrificed on the altar of Zeus,' Heracles tells him.

Joshua is *horrified*. 'You can't slaughter a *thousand* animals!'

Stavros looks at him as though he's gone insane. 'Zeus must be pleased with the sacrifice or the Games will be cursed.'

Josh shakes his head. Going to church on Sunday morning is *kids' stuff* compared to this!

In the searing heat of the morning sun the crowd processes towards the great temple of Zeus where Heracles approaches the high altar. Shouting and cracking their whips the slaves drive the oxen forwards. Confused and afraid the beasts panic, but the slaves whip them towards Heracles who is holding a huge silver axe with a gleaming sharp edge. One by one he slaughters every single ox until the grass at his feet is slippery with their blood. The air is loud with the bleating and grunting of terrified animals, the smell of spilt bowels is nauseous, the heat is stifling – it is the grimmest spectacle Joshua has ever lived through, but nobody else seems to mind. The crowd nod in approval as Heracles carries the thighbones of the slaughtered beasts up the steps to the high altar where they are burnt as a ceremonial sacrifice. What remains of the stinking one thousand carcasses is carried off by slaves to provide meat for the evening feast.

When all is done the crowd quickly disperse, eager to secure their seats in the stadium where the foot races will soon start. Stavros hurries after Theagenes who is returning to the gymnasium with the athletes to make last-minute preparations. Heracles stands brooding over the smouldering sacrificial fire, staring up at the statue of his father. Slipping in the pools of blood Josh creeps towards him and gasps in amazement. From where he was standing with the twenty thousand spectators he was unable to see the splendour of the high altar where the seated figure of Zeus, beautifully crafted from wood, gold and ivory, towers thirteen metres high. The god is adorned with a crown made of fine gold olive leaves. Cupped in his right hand is a delicate statue of Nike, the goddess of Victory; in his left hand he grasps a sceptre. In a rapt trance Heracles speaks to the statue.

'Lord God, tell me what I should do.'

From behind the plumes of smoke a mighty voice speaks out.

'Fulfil your destiny, my son.'

'But I am weary, Lord.'

'Soon you will rest in the Fields of Joy.'

'And the boy, Joshua?' Heracles asks.

'He must travel to Hades where his father awaits him.'

'I have protected him from an evil force. Who will take my place?'

'I will send my son Hermes the Messenger to travel beside him.'

'Why not Athene? She will give him wisdom.'

A low rumble followed by a blinding zigzag makes Joshua jump in terror.

'Do not question *my* wisdom, Heracles!' growls Zeus. 'The boy will meet my daughter Athene later, at her temple in Athens.'

Heracles bows low and salutes his father then turns to find Joshua standing behind him with tears streaming down his face.

'Is Zeus telling you you're going to die?' he cries.

Heracles hurries forwards to embrace him in his huge arms.

'Our destinies are taking us along different tracks, Joshua, but we will always be friends.'

'How can we be friends if you're *dead*?' sobs Joshua.

Heracles squats beside the devastated boy and speaks to him gently.

'You of *all* people should know that death is not an ending. We will meet again, Joshua, in the afterlife, which is untouched by fear and pain.'

Joshua thumps the ground in frustration. 'But this world, our world, is *real*,' he protests. 'At least I can feel you and see you here.'

'That's your reality *now*, Joshua.'

'I don't want you to die,' Josh replies angrily. 'I need you!'

Heracles grips his hand firmly in his. 'My spirit will always be beside you. I promise.'

In sombre silence they return to the Olympic village where they part ways – Heracles to the gymnasium and Joshua to the stadium.

The stadium is packed with twenty thousand spectators all pressed together on the high bank built along the one hundred and ninety-two metre track. The heat inside the stadium is intense but fortunately there's a channel of water running along the edge of the track where the spectators and the athletes can cool themselves. The runners for the first foot race are already in position, with their feet gripping the grooves at the starting line. At a signal from one of the judges they sprint down one length of the stadium. Their speed is phenomenal and the crowd go wild as a youth who is clearly the favourite zips by.

'Go Leonidas – GO!'

With his dark hair streaming behind him Leonidas from Rhodes moves like a young gazelle and finishes first, winning the heat. The second, third and fourth heat quickly follow, then it's the final. As the athletes line up you could hear a pin drop among the tense crowd. At the judge's command the sprinters take off and Leonidas is like a blur on the track. When he reaches the finishing line the spectators go crazy and continue to cheer wildly as he's crowned with the winner's olive wreath. Just as everybody is starting to get their breath, the next race starts. Leonidas reappears looking as fresh as a daisy for a two-length sprint of the stadium. With effortless ease he wins the first heat then waits by the water channel for the other heats to be run. He then proceeds to win the final and receives his second crown of victory. Suddenly the crowd go very still. It's the sort of atmosphere that Joshua has only ever experienced during a penalty shoot out in a World Cup match. He looks at the intense faces around him.

'What's going on?' he asks the burly man beside him.

'The next race is the long-distance race,' he replies. 'The contestants have to cover twenty-four lengths of the stadium. If Leonidas from Rhodes wins this race he will become the Triastes.'

Josh looks blank.

'The three-timer,' the man explains.

'Ah, a hat trick!' exclaims Josh.

The long-distance race begins and the competitors set off at a steady, even pace, knowing they've got a long way to run in the baking afternoon heat. After the nineteenth lap two-thirds of the athletes start to speed up but Leonidas maintains the same steady rhythm. It's only towards the end of the twenty-second lap that the youth gathers speed and starts overtaking everybody in his path. As he enters into the last lap and starts sprinting towards the finishing line with no other contestant in sight, shivers creep up and down Josh's spine. He's never seen *anything* as beautiful since Michael Owen scored *that* hat trick against Germany in the World Cup Qualifier in 2001! Leonidas receives his *third* crown of victory and goes into the history books. He is the supreme TRIASTES, an athlete for ever after worshipped as a hero!

Dazed with hunger and excitement Josh gulps from the channel of water in the stadium then cups some in his hand for Muck to lap up. The heat of the day is fading and thousands of people are slowly dispersing from the stadium and heading for the hippodrome where the horse-racing events are taking place.

Josh finds Heracles in the Palaestra.

'Stavros has gone off to eat the sacrificial oxen,' Heracles tells him. 'Are you hungry?'

The smell of roasting meat is thick in the air. Josh's stomach heaves as he recalls the morning's slaughter and the grass under his feet running with warm blood.

'Yes, but not for meat,' he replies.

'Come, I'll catch you a trout for supper,' says Heracles.

Though the sun is setting, the heat of the day hangs heavy in the air. Josh flings his chiton to the ground and throws himself head first into the cool, clear waters of the babbling River Alpheus. As he dives underwater and glories in the tingling cold, Heracles searches for trout. When he finds a big fat one basking in the shadows he tickles its belly until it lies still in his hands, then he quickly lifts it out of the water and kills it with a sharp blow to the head.

'Now we'll gut it,' he says.

Joshua surfaces from the water and calls out, 'I'm the expert at that – leave it to me!'

Josh knows exactly how to gut fish. With a flourish he sticks a sharp knife into the fish's stomach, which he splits wide open, then deftly flips out the gleaming innards. Heracles watches him, impressed.

'With that kind of precision you'd make a fine sacrificial high priest in the temple of Zeus,' he says.

Joshua shakes his head. 'After what I witnessed this morning, no thanks!'

'Where did you learn that?' Heracles asks.

'My mum,' Josh replies. 'She opened a chip shop after my dad died.'

'She has not remarried?'

Josh shakes his head. 'No, though the meat-pie man has asked her twice.'

'Is she unwed because she is a barren and beyond her child-bearing years?' Heracles asks solemnly.

Joshua bursts out laughing. 'She's unmarried because she doesn't fancy anybody, and me and my brother would have a fit if she got pregnant!'

'Women should bear as many children as possible.'

'*WHY*?'

'Because only the strongest survive – the weakest die. In Sparta the father tests a baby's strength by rubbing it with icy water, wine and urine.'

'YUK! I think I'd rather die than be rubbed in wee!'

'If the child is weak the father leaves it on the hillside where it will die of starvation or be eaten by wolves.'

'Pity nobody did that with my brother!' jokes Josh.

Chatting easily they bake the fish over a fire and eat it with bread and black olives. Heracles adds a bundle of twigs to the crackling fire and Muck settles down for the night, curled up beside her master.

'This is our final night together,' Heracles says.

Despite the heat from the fire, Josh shivers as if someone were walking over his grave. On the edge of tears he blurts out:

'I'm scared of being on my own.'

'You will not be alone. Zeus will send his son, Hermes the Messenger, to guide you through the next part of your journey.'

'But I don't know where I'm going!' Joshua cries in frustration. 'I don't even know where Hades is!'

'Trust in the Immortals – they will guide you. Now listen closely to what I have to tell you, Joshua, and follow my advice. Otherwise you will never even find the Underworld.'

Anxious not to miss a word Josh inches closer to Heracles.

'You will discover the entrance to the Underworld in the Ionian Sea, quite close to the island of Sicily. In a deep wild gorge the River of Flaming Fire and the River of Lamentation converge in a huge torrent of foaming water. Close to their convergence is a cave hung with shimmering stone. This is the entry to the Underworld. Steep winding paths will lead you into the bowels of the earth where the Styx – the River of Hate – flows.'

Joshua shivers at Heracles' vivid description and his skin creeps in fear.

'On the banks of the river you will see the souls of the dead waiting to be ferried over by Charon the Ferryman. On the other side, standing by the gates to the Underworld is Cerberus, the three-headed hound who guards the entry.

'How do I get past a three-headed hound?' Josh asks.

'You will be given the means to do that in the latter part of your journey,' Heracles tells him.

Josh shakes his head in bewilderment. 'Another mystery!'

'Where is the white barley that Tiresias gave you?'

Josh hands over the purse with the barley and the coin inside.

'On the banks of the Styx you must dig a trench as long and wide as your forearm.'

'WHY?'

'Because you have to make a libation to the King and Queen of the Underworld,' Heracles explains. 'You must go around the trench and pour in offerings to the dead.'

'Not oxen's thighbones?' Josh asks nervously.

'No, sweet wine, honey, milk and water.'

Josh is seriously puzzled.

'Where am I going to pick up stuff like that in the bowels of the earth?'

'It will be given to you.'

'Mystery number two!' he jokes.

'Don't make light of what I have to say,' Heracles warns darkly. 'Make one wrong move in the Underworld and you will join the ranks of the dead on the banks of the Styx.'

Joshua quickly apologises. 'Sorry. What do I do after I've dug the trench and poured in all the stuff you said?'

'You must sacrifice a ram and a black ewe and pour their blood into the ground.'

'I don't want to kill anything!'

'The sacrifice *has* to be made to Hades and Persephone or you will not be allowed entry.' Heracles pauses and stares at Josh. '*Promise* me you'll do it?'

Joshua hesitates. 'What's a black ewe?'

'A female sheep. Don't you have them in Hyperborea?'

Rather embarrassed by his ignorance Josh nods and says, 'Yes. I didn't know they were called ewes!' Then he asks a question that he dreads hearing the answer to.

'How will I kill them?'

'You'll cut their throats with this knife.'

Heracles removes a belt from his waist; on it hangs a silver knife in a scabbard. 'It's seen me through my twelve labours – it'll slit through a sheep's throat like silk.'

Feeling very queasy Josh secures the leather belt around his waist but half of it dangles on the floor. 'It's too big!' he laughs.

Heracles takes the knife from the scabbard and chops off the surplus length. 'I'd forgotten you were half my size.'

'More like a quarter!'

'Is there anything else you need to ask me?' says Heracles.

Joshua nods. 'I've been worrying about this since I started my journey. How can I meet my father if he's dead?'

'Your father is an Immortal. He lives eternally with the Legends in the Fields of Joy. He will be waiting for you, I promise.'

'Is Leirtod a Legend?'

'He was a great Legend when the world was young. He was Lumaluce's seer and guide. He knew the movements of the earth and the stars. He knew ancient languages and investigated the world of science and mathematics. Leirtod gave all this knowledge to Lumaluce, but then he grew jealous of his protégé's popularity among the people. Leirtod resented him and conspired with the generals to murder Lumaluce, but they refused to harm a hair of his head. Leirtod was pronounced a traitor and has forever since slunk in the shadows, conspiring to revenge himself on your father whom he cannot touch.'

'So now he's decided to have his revenge through ME!'

'We are all trying to protect you, Joshua.'

'But you're leaving me!' cries Josh in a panic.

'The Winged Messenger, Hermes, will take my place and guide you to the sacred shrine of Athene, who will lead you to Hades.' Heracles' voice drops to a whisper. 'Be careful of Hermes, he is full of mischief and will be less watchful than me.'

Josh sighs sadly. 'I'll miss you,' he murmurs.

Heracles gives him a hug. 'You may not feel my arm around you but My spirit will walk with you, little Hyperborean.'

The following morning the three friends part ways for ever. Stavros remains in Olympia, Heracles heads north for Arcadia and Joshua sets off on the road for Hades!

CHAPTER TEN

On the Road with Hermes

Clutching Muck in his arms Joshua walks down a dusty track that seems to end on the far horizon.

'I hope this is the right road, otherwise it's going to be a long walk back,' he tells the pup.

'AWWKK!'

'Mate!' cries Josh as the big seagull swoops down and settles on his shoulder where he gently nibbles his ear! 'I am so *glad* to see you!'

'Why are you talking to a bird?' a voice behind him snaps.

Josh whizzes round and gasps in amazement as he comes face to face with a slender youth fluttering slightly above ground level with tiny wings on his heels.

'Er, he's my friend, my guide,' he replies awkwardly.

'I am your guide for the moment, so lose the bird!'

Mate needs no telling. Squawking indignantly he flies up, and just to make his feelings completely clear he relieves himself directly over Hermes' head. The offending blob is about to plop on to the young god's head, but Hermes' waves a stick and it explodes into a shower of stars. Mate hastily flies off before the same thing happens to him!

'How did you do that?'

'I blasted it with my moly stick!' Hermes thrusts a stick in front of Joshua.

'A twig!'

'It's not a twig – it's moly and it's magic, you mortal fool!'

'What else can it do?'

Hermes looks around and catches sight of little Muck scampering on the path. He waves the stick and the puppy is instantly transformed into a piglet.

'Oink! Oink!' goes Muck.

Joshua is horrified. 'AHH! Change her back!'

With a wave of his moly stick Hermes brings the puppy back to normal. Petrified she scrabbles at Josh's legs until he scoops her up and pops her into his pouch, where she buries down as far as she can go.

'I don't think she likes you very much,' says Josh.

'It was you who asked me to demonstrate the power of moly. Can we get a move on, mortal? Hippodrax is on our heels in hot pursuit of you.'

Joshua goes white with fear. 'Is he close?'

'I should think so,' says Hermes, giving the little wings on his feet a flutter. 'Leirtod knows you left Olympia so he won't be far behind.'

Josh breaks into a sprint to keep up with his guide.

'I am Hermes, the Winged Messenger of Zeus. He sent me to take care of you because you are the son of Lumaluce of whom the Immortals are very fond.'

'Thank you,' Josh splutters as he runs beside speedy little god.

'Don't thank me. I hate mortals, so tedious and *slow*.'

Sweat is bursting out on Josh's brow as he now races to keep up with the impatient Hermes.

'But Zeus insisted so here I am. Oh, get a move on, boy!'

Hermes leads Joshua into a rugged valley dotted with ancient oak trees and fragrant with the smell of wild thyme and fennel. Among the trees graze wild goats, who bleat indignantly as they pass by.

'Baaa!' bleats Hermes in a grumpy billy goat's ear.

The goat turns to butt him but Hermes gives him a tap with his moly stick and turns him into a frog.

'Glub, glub, glub!' goes the astonished goat.

'Stop playing tricks and turn him back,' begs Joshua.

'Oh, you are a spoilsport,' says Hermes as he waves his moly stick and the goat reappears. 'If you don't like practical jokes you'd better watch out for my half-brother, Apollo. He's the God of Transformations and he's around here somewhere. I can hear his music.'

As he speaks, sweet music drifts down the mountainside and mingles with the sound of the bells tinkling around the goats' necks. Suddenly one of the rams charges at Josh and butts him hard in the stomach.

'OUCH!' he yells as he falls to the ground and cuts his knee on a sharp rock.

'Sorry,' says the goat who tripped him up.

'What's going on?' asks Josh in complete astonishment.

Hermes waves his moly stick and a beautiful young man appears carrying a lyre and a silver bow. Over his shoulder is slung a quiver full of glittering silver arrows. He smiles at Joshua. 'I'm Apollo the Sun God and the God of Transformations – can you sing for me, boy?'

Joshua gulps nervously. He doesn't want to say no in case he offends the God of Transformations, who might on a whim transform him into an elephant!

'I can sing "Danny Boy".'

'Then sing!'

Josh takes a deep breath and haltingly starts to sing 'Danny Boy', his mum's favourite song, which drifts out over the beautiful countryside scaring the goats away!

'Good,' says Apollo as Joshua finishes. 'Let's try singing it together.'

'Can we save the entertainment for later?' snaps Hermes. 'I've got the beast from hell on my tail and I'd like to get safely undercover by nightfall.'

'I'll walk along with you,' says Apollo. 'Two gods are better than one when it comes to warding off demons.'

They hurry through the sweet-smelling valley but stop when they see a group of pretty nymphs dancing on the hillside. The maidens are surrounded by sheep and lambs which bleat in fear and hurry to their mothers as they approach.

'Well, well, what have we here?' exclaims Apollo.

'We haven't got time to chat up nymphs,' says Hermes. 'Joshua is on the run!'

'You can run – I'll stay,' says Apollo.

'Nymphs are afraid of men. If you go near them they'll run away,' warns Hermes.

'They'll come flocking to me, just you see,' says Apollo.

With a wink he turns himself into a tortoise and crawls towards the nymphs who rush over to admire him. One picks him up and kisses his cute little nose, another presses him to her bosom. Hermes shakes his head.

'Unbelievable!' he mutters. 'Come boy, this is not for your innocent eyes!'

Joshua obediently hurries after Hermes, who suddenly stops and sniffs the air. 'Hippodrax is close by – I can smell him. HIDE!'

Hermes shoves Joshua behind a clump of thick rosemary bushes. 'Wait here until I get back,' he commands and in a flash he's gone! Muck immediately pops out of her pouch and whines for her tea.

'Be quiet,' Josh tells her firmly but the hungry pup yaps even louder. 'How can you think of food at a time like this?' Josh asks.

Seeing as there's nothing forthcoming from her master, Muck leaps from her pouch and scampers under the bushes.

'Come back!' he hisses.

In answer Muck yaps excitedly. Joshua scrambles after her on his hands and knees. '*Please* shut up,' he implores.

'Hippodrax will hear you.'

Thinking they're playing a game the mischievous pup runs clears of the bushes and scampers into a nearby cave.

'Ruff! Rufff! Ruffff!'

Still on his hands and knees Josh follows her into the gloomy cave where he crawls slap-bang into something very big and very hairy.

'AHHH!' he screams as he stares into the demonic face of Hippodrax!

Squealing the centaur canters around the cave, demonstrating his ferocity. Josh cowers in terror as the beast rears and kicks then charges towards him. Grabbing the trembling pup he skips out of the way of his glancing hooves and desperately looks around for shelter. Suddenly he spots a narrow crevice, which he squeezes into. Muck wriggles in protest as she's squashed up against the hard rock face.

'It's better in here than out there with a raving monster!' Josh mutters as Hippodrax's hooves smash against the rock face. BOOM! Just as Josh is thinking he's going to get his head kicked in, a roar fills the cave and a huge black thing hurls itself down on top of Hippodrax. It's a mountain bear with teeth like razors and paws as big as saucepans. Growling and snarling it clings to Hippodrax and bites his neck. Grunting in pain Hippodrax bucks the bear off his back and charges out of the cave. Josh peeps out of his hiding place and stares at the big black bear. Has he got rid of one monster only to face another? The bear sits on his haunches growling at him, then to Josh's amazement it starts to hum 'Danny Boy'.

'YOU!' gasps Josh as the bear is replaced by Apollo.

'I thought you might need a little help!'

'How did you do that?'

'Easy – I'm a god of disguises. Now where's Hermes and what was he doing leaving you here on your own?'

'He said he could smell Hippodrax and went off to find him.'

'I bet he's visiting those charming nymphs!' says Apollo as he springs to his feet. 'I'm hungry – let's catch supper.'

Josh nods eagerly – a close scrape with certain death has given him a heck of an appetite!

As Apollo roasts a wild deer on a wooden spit he's made from tree saplings, Josh says, 'You know, while I was squashed up in the crevice with Hippodrax beating against the rock less than a metre away, I suddenly thought of Odysseus.'

'A great hero,' says Apollo as he adds more twigs to the blaze. 'Tell me a story from the Odyssey while I cook your supper.'

'You must know the Odyssey backwards,' exclaims Josh.

'Of course! But if a tale is good we Ancient Greeks like to hear it *over and over* again.'

Joshua thinks it's bizarre that he, an inadequate mortal, is regaling a god with a story he's never even spoken out loud before.

'Well …' he begins hesitantly.

'Don't be timid, boy!' Apollo chides him. 'Tell your tale with pride.'

Realising he's got to give it some welly, Joshua takes a deep breath and begins boldly.

'Odysseus was one of the Greek warriors who built the Wooden Horse of Troy. After the Greeks beat the Trojans in one of the bloodiest battles in history, Odysseus and his crew set off for Ithaca, their home.'

'Don't forget how angry Poseidon the Sea God was,' Apollo reminds him as he sprinkles wild thyme on to the deer's crackling carcass.

'I was coming to that!' Josh replies. 'Poseidon was furious with the Greeks for burning his favourite city to the ground, but he was particularly angry with Odysseus who had come up with the cunning plot of the Trojan Horse in the first place.'

'Smart idea,' chuckles Apollo.

'Poseidon blew Odysseus and his men around the seas of the world. They went here, there and everywhere, fought demons, monsters, witches – and then they were blown on to the island of Polyphemus, the giant one-eyed Cyclops who unfortunately happened to be the son of Poseidon.'

'Double trouble!' says Apollo who's clearly enjoying the tale.

'Odysseus took twelve of his men—'

'And a skin of his strongest wine – don't forget the wine,' Apollo chides him.

Joshua wants to say, 'Am I telling this story or you?' But he doesn't want to upset the god of disguises who after all has just saved his life.

'He took a skin of very strong wine and entered the Cyclops' cave while Polyphemus was out grazing his sheep on the hillside. The cave was full of sheep's cheeses, which the crew longed to eat but Odysseus forbade them, he said it would be rude to take the food without it being offered by the owner.

'An upright Greek,' says Apollo. 'I wish there were more like him!'

'When Polyphemus returned with his sheep in the evening, he slammed a huge boulder over the entrance, which meant that Odysseus and his men couldn't get out. But heroes don't panic!'

'Heroes *never* panic,' Apollo assures him.

'Odysseus approached the Cyclops and spoke politely to him.'

'Fine manners are wasted on a one-eyed monster!' says Apollo dismissively.

'"Sir, we are strangers in your country. Please give us food and shelter for the night."

'"Strangers!" cried the Cyclops. "Ha ha! I'll eat you all for supper."

'With a roar he chased the terrified crew around his cave and grabbed six of them. Odysseus watched in horror as the Cyclops dropped the screaming men into his mouth and swallowed them whole! He would have eaten them all but

Odysseus approached him once more, this time with the skin of strong wine.'

'A cunning man, for a mortal,' says Apollo with respect.

'Odysseus handed him the wine, which the Cyclops guzzled back, then he fell into a drunken stupor. As he lay on the floor of the cave snoring his head off, Odysseus grabbed a long piece of olive wood and started to sharpen it. His men were frightened ... why was their leader whittling wood at a time of great crisis? When the end of the olive was sharp and pointed Odysseus gave it to his men and told them to put it into the fire and turn it until the tip was red hot. The men did as he instructed then he told them to shove the stick into the Cyclop's eye!

'I do *love* this bit!' says Apollo, hanging on Josh's every word.

'Odysseus's men refused.

'"We can't do that – he'll kill us!"

'"He'll kill us anyway," said Odysseus. "When I say three – do it!"

'Trembling in fear the crew approached the Cyclops.

'"One, two, THREE!" yelled Odysseus.

'The men charged at the Cyclops and rammed the red-hot stick into his single eye.

'"AAAAAAH!" he howled in agony but the crew kept on turning the stick inside his bleeding socket. Shouting and screaming the Cyclops lurched to his feet and tried to chase them but of course he couldn't see them. Odysseus raced to the entrance of the cave and tried to shift the boulder that blocked their exit. He couldn't move it! The crew hurried to help him but not even their combined strength could shift the boulder. They had blinded the Cyclops and now they were stuck inside the cave with him!'

'Could things have got any worse?' says Apollo gleefully.

'The long night finally ended and as dawn broke, the sheep inside the cave started to bleat.

'"Baaa! Baaaa!"

'"Ah, my little ones," called the Cyclops. "You must go out and graze in the bright new day that I shall never see."

'He drew back the huge boulder and some of the sheep ran out into the sunny meadow. The Cyclops called to the ones that remained. "Come my pretty ones!"

'"We'll never get out with Polyphemus blocking the entrance," whispered one the crew.

'Then Odysseus had a brainwave.

'"Pretend to be sheep!" he whispered. "Grab some sheep and hide underneath them."

'"How?" the crew asked.

'"Tie yourselves underneath the sheeps' bellies," Odysseus replied.

'The crew chased after the sheep but Odysseus spotted a big old ram. He crept up on it then grabbed it and using the belt from his chiton he tied himself to the ram.

'"Baaa!" bleated the ram crossly.

'When Polyphemus heard the ram he called out.

'"Come, my beauty!"

'The ram trotted over to him and Polyphemus fondly stoked his thick fleece. Odysseus held his breath as he felt the Cyclops' huge fingertips touch the top of his hair.'

'Hahhh!' gasps Apollo as he shivers in delight. 'You tell a good tale, mortal.'

'The Cyclops patted his favourite ram then sent him out to graze in the sunny meadow. The second Odysseus was out of the cave, he untied the belt and leapt free of the ram. One by one his men came out of the cave under the bellies of the frisking sheep.

'"To the ship!" yelled Odysseus.

'Yelling and screaming with relief that they were alive, they raced back to the ship and within minutes they were sailing away from that wretched island, leaving blind Polyphemus behind them.'

'Cunning Odysseus to outwit a Cyclops,' says Apollo. 'But he paid dearly for his deed. Polyphemus was the son of Poseidon, who cast Odysseus and his crew adrift for another ten long years.' He hands Joshua a leg of herb-scented roasted deer. 'Eat, boy – and thank you for entertaining me!'

Hermes returns and hungrily rips into the wild deer.

'Where've you been?' asks Apollo. 'I've just chased Hippodrax down the mountainside *and* made your tea.' 'I went for a walk,' says Hermes moodily. 'I'm fed up with babysitting mortal fools!'

113

'What're you going to do with the boy?' Apollo asks, as if Joshua were a piece of left luggage at a railway station.

'He's on a journey to find his illustrious father, Lumaluce, but first I've got to take him to meet Athene.'

Apollo is impressed. 'But Lumaluce's a Legend and dwells in the Underworld.'

'I know that!' growls Hermes impatiently. 'It is because of the Immortals' great love of Lumaluce that they guard the boy as he travels to his father. First Tiresias, then the worthy Heracles, who hardly took his eyes off the child for a second, and now *me*.'

Josh shuffles uncomfortably. 'I'm sorry to put you to so much trouble …'

'Oh, get lost!' says Hermes rudely. 'I could be up on Mount Olympus eating ambrosia instead of stuck here gnawing on a scraggy deer's leg.' In disgust he throws the bone to the ground. 'Once I've dropped him off at the Parthenon, Athene plans to give him wisdom. Hah! That's a joke. He is so stupid!'

Feeling awkward, and terrified of being turned into a grass snake or a fruit bat by grumpy Hermes, Joshua slips away with Muck and goes to sit under a tree. Here he feeds the pup little shreds of roasted deer meat which she greatly appreciates. Suddenly Hermes' shadow falls over Joshua, causing him to jump in fright.

'It is the custom for guests once fed to entertain their hosts.'

Josh's jaw drops. How can HE entertain two moody gods?

'Er, what would you like me to do?'

'Can you dance?' Hermes asks hopefully.

There's no way that Josh is going to get up and dance the funky stomp in front of two Immortals!

'No!'

'Do you know any poetry?' asks Apollo.

Joshua thinks hard. He knows a couple of dirty limericks and a soppy poem about rabbits.

'No!' he says emphatically.

'What *can* you do?' sneers Hermes.

Josh has a brainwave. 'CHARADES! I can play charades!'

Feeling nervous Joshua stands before the gods and makes the gesture for a book,

'What are you doing?' snaps Hermes impatiently.

'It's a book,' says Joshua then remembers they don't have such a thing in Ancient Greece! 'It's the name of a story,' he explains as he holds up five fingers. 'There are five words in the title.'

'Then it's a very short story, certainly not a legend,' jokes Apollo.

Having established the ground rules Josh proceeds to mime 'The Wooden Horse of Troy', which baffles the gods who make all sorts of wild guesses.

Josh completely cracks up when Hermes cries out, 'The Galloping Trojan Oak Tree!'

'Rubbish, there's no such story as the "Galloping Trojan Oak Tree!"' scoffs Apollo.

Eager to avoid an argument Josh interrupts their bickering and says, 'I'll give you another clue.' He neighs shrilly.

'Ah! A horse,' say Hermes.

'But *what* sort of a horse?' puzzles Apollo.

In desperation Joshua bangs his head against the nearest tree.

'It's a wooden horse!' shouts Hermes as he picks up the clue.

'The Wooden Horse of Troy!' yells Apollo.

'Yes!' cries Joshua.

Apollo and Hermes love charades so much that they beg Josh to play it over and over again until finally he uses up his entire stock of Greek epics. Apollo says he will repay his guest's courtesy with a story about his son, Orpheus.

'Listen carefully, mortal. This ancient legend may be of use to you when you journey into the Underworld.'

Hermes excuses himself and says he'll go and scout around to make sure that Hippodrax hasn't returned. The second he's gone Apollo winks at Josh and says, 'He'll be nipping down the mountainside to see the pretty little nymphs sleeping in their fragrant bowers.'

Suddenly afraid that Apollo might run off and join him, Joshua urges him to begin the story.

'*I* am the greatest musician among the gods, but in the mortal world my son Orpheus was supreme. He could sing and play the lyre to lull dragons to sleep. Orpheus fell in love with a beautiful girl called Eurydice, who unfortunately was bitten by a viper and died. Orpheus was inconsolable. It was terrible to watch his grief. He decided he would go to Hades and bring his beloved Eurydice back.'

Josh sits bolt upright.

'Did Orpheus know where to find the entrance to Hades?' he asks.

'Yes, every Greek knows that the Underworld can be found in a gorge near Sicily in the Ionian Sea, where the River of Flaming Fire and the River of Lamentation converge. On the site is a cave, hung with shimmering stone. It is unmistakable. Inside, a steep path leads directly down to the River Styx.'

Joshua is relieved that Apollo's description matches that of Heracles.

'So Orpheus set off with his golden lyre slung over his shoulder. He travelled across the Ionian Sea to the place where the rivers converge and found the entrance to the cave. He followed the path down to the River Styx where he found Charon, the ferryman, loading those whose time had come to cross over from life into death. Orpheus knew it would not be easy to persuade Charon to take a living body, but a melodious note on his lyre brought a smile to the grim ferryman's face and he happily rowed him across the river. Waiting on the other side was Cerberus, the three-headed monstrous dog who guards the gates of hell.'

An ice-cold shiver slithers down Joshua's spine – he has all this yet to come and he doesn't even have a good singing voice! For a split second he deeply regrets not taking Dido's advice and joining the school choir.

'Boys don't sing,' he'd told her arrogantly.

Dido had scoffed at his ignorance.

'Boys *do* sing, you nerd! They've been singing for the kings and queens of Europe for centuries. Look at Shakespeare, Orlando Gibbons, Kings College Choir.'

Instead of doing the sensible thing and giving it a go, Joshua had stuck to his prejudices and refused point blank. If he'd known then that a fine singing voice could save his life, he might have thought twice about it.

Apollo continues. 'Cerberus growled but as Orpheus strummed his lyre the dog stopped snarling, and – like Charon – was charmed by his music and allowed the stranger to pass. Tiresias stood at the gates of the Underworld to greet Orpheus.'

'I know him!' cries Joshua. 'He made me fill terracotta pots with water, just to test how bright I was. I don't think he was very impressed by me, actually.'

Deep in his story Apollo ignores Josh's interruption.

'Orpheus entered the gates of hell where Persephone, queen of the Underworld, was waiting for him. Her heart was moved by Orpheus's great love for Eurydice and she allowed him to take his beloved back to the mortal world. "There is one condition," said Persephone. "She must follow behind you as you leave the Underworld. If you should turn around to look at her before she reaches the upper world, Eurydice must return here *for ever*." Orpheus promptly agreed to all that Persephone said.

'He and Eurydice left the Underworld and started the

long climb up to the surface of the earth. Orpheus never looked back. Up and up he went until he could see daylight, then he stopped and listened ... he could hear footsteps behind him but were they *really* Eurydice? He turned to check and as he looked she faded away. He had done the one thing Persephone had told him not to do – he had looked back and lost his love for ever.'

At the end of his sad story Apollo turns to Joshua, who sighs heavily.

'You Ancient Greeks don't go in for happy endings, do you?'

Early the following morning they say farewell to Apollo, who, before he transforms himself into a parrot, hands Joshua his lyre.

'Remember how Orpheus charmed Charon and Cerberus with his music and singing?'

'But I can neither sing nor play!' he blurts out.

'Then start practising, mortal, or die!'

Their last sight of Apollo is of him winging into the nymphs' fragrant bower, where he playfully nibbles the ears of the pretty ladies who fondly stroke his tail feathers. Clearly envious of Apollo and bored with his task of babysitting a mortal, Hermes keeps disappearing into thin air then reappearing a mile up the track urging Josh to quicken his pace.

In one of the Messenger God's frequent absences, Mate

swoops down and perches on Josh's shoulder. The seagull curiously cocks his head to one side as Muck wriggles out of his pouch and growls at him.

'Cool it, pup,' laughs Josh. 'I don't want you scaring off my only friend from the twenty-first century.' He smiles up at the big bird. 'From the moment Mate turned up at Shakespeare's Chippy strange things started happening to me. You've guided me here, Mate ... I wonder if you'll guide me home again?' Josh murmurs thoughtfully.

'Talking to *birds* again?' scoffs a voice behind him.

The sight of Hermes sends Mate swooping off in alarm while little Muck quickly nose-dives back into the safety of her pouch. Josh grins.

'Animals *really* don't like being near you,' he remarks.

'Children ... animals, they're so boring,' snaps Hermes as he irritably shoves some sweet honey cakes into Josh's hands. 'Eat these. Maybe they'll make you walk *faster!*'

By nightfall they reach the outskirts of Athens where the streets are thronged with pedestrians and traders calling their wares. Joshua's nostrils are assailed by the delicious smell of hot spicy sausages. Sniffing the air like a hungry dog he follows the smell to a makeshift barbecue where a woman is doing a brisk trade in grilled sausage and hot barley bread. A plume of smoke obscures the faces of the waiting customers but when it clears Josh finds himself looking at Stavros!

'Haven't we met like this before?' says Stav, recalling their first meeting in Zachynthus.

Josh flings his arms around his friend and hugs him tightly. 'What're you doing in Athens?'

'Theagenes sent me to pick up some ointments for bruises and sprains.' Stav holds up a basket containing flasks of oily liquid. 'He swears this stuff heals everything.'

At the sound of Stav's voice Muck springs out of his pouch and yaps ecstatically.

'Hey, mutt! You've grown,' says Stav as he feeds the dog a morsel of sausage. Muck wolfs down the tasty meat then suddenly her eyes widen. 'Just watch those spices kick in!' laughs Stav.

'She needs some water,' says Josh.

He hurries over to a nearby fountain where Muck gulps back mouthfuls of cool water. As Josh stands waiting for her to finish, Hermes, who has become invisible in the busy square, snaps in his ear.

'Get a move on, you witless mortal.'

'Yes, yes,' Josh replies but Stav comes up and throws an arm around his shoulder

'Let's have a nice, *long* chat before I go.'

Joshua can't think of anything more he'd like to do but he can feel Hermes poking him in the back.

'I'm warning you boy – don't loiter!' hisses the furious Winged Messenger.

'Stav, I've *really* got to go!'

'Not until I've told you about this *amazing* Spartan athlete who's just turned up in Olympia – I tell you he's the size of a house!'

As Josh dithers between invisible Hermes on one side and Stav on the other, Muck suddenly has a fit! The hot spice in the back of her throat seems to send her into a frenzy of wild excitement and she starts to race around the square like she's got the devil on her tail.

'Muck! Come back!' Josh yells as she scampers head-long into the street sellers. One of them furiously kicks out at the dog, sending her flying through the air. The two boys rush forward to catch her but Josh trips over Stav's feet and falls headlong on to a makeshift fruit stall which collapses under his weight. Stav grabs Muck before she gets another kick in the ribs and Josh, with bunches of grapes draped around his face, drags himself up to face the stall owner.

'S … sorry,' he starts to apologise.

'THIEVES!' she screams. 'Call the guard!'

As the boys are hauled off protesting their innocence, Joshua looks around for Hermes, his Immortal protector, who of course is nowhere to be seen!

CHAPTER ELEVEN

Slammed Up with Pythagoras!

Stavros and Joshua are thrown into separate cells and left alone. In the stifling gloom Josh clutches Muck close to him.

'Duh-brain! This is all your fault!' he scolds the pup, who cringes with fear. Feeling her shaking in his arms Josh hasn't the heart to go on. 'Don't worry, we'll be out of here soon,' he murmurs.

'I wouldn't bet on it!' a horribly familiar voice rasps in his ears.

Joshua's heart contracts in sheer terror. It's the worst-case scenario – he's slammed up in a dark confined space with a madman whose sole intent is *his* death!

'Joshua Cross,' Leirtod savours every syllable of the name he loathes. 'What better place to slit your skinny white throat than here in the dark. Nobody will open the door till morning, by which time your blood will have oozed all over the prison floor. It will be a sight to break your father's heart.'

Joshua stiffens as he hears a rustle. He can't see a thing but all his senses tell him that Leirtod is reaching for the jewelled silver knife that flashed before his eyes in the moonlight only a few nights ago. Suddenly words spurt from his mouth that startle him with their boldness.

'Tell me about your fight with my father.'

There's a pause – one in which Joshua does not know exactly where the knife hovers – then Leirtod laughs hollowly.

'Why not?'

Joshua lets out a long slow breath and hopes that the story about to unfold will be the longest in history.

'I was your father's seer and he was my fine student. As a boy he looked like you – white hair, silver eyes and an intellect that was insatiable. He had the face of an angel and the body of a god. He shone with an inner light as if blessed by a great spirit. The people loved him and gave him the name "Lumaluce", the bright shining one. I taught him everything – literature, philosophy, arithmetic, geometry, music, cosmology and theology. He was *astonishingly* bright and stored up all the knowledge I gave him. I was immensely proud of him, but as he grew into manhood I began to hate him. I had given him *all* that I possessed but the people loved HIM – not ME! I decided I had to destroy him or he would take away my glory. Twice I tried to poison him and failed, so I approached the war generals with a lie. I told them that Lumaluce was planning an uprising. They refused to believe me but I had contrived a plan, which convinced them. Lumaluce was arrested and brought to trial. When he stood before the war generals the truth shone around him like a luminescent aura – he was palpably innocent and I was palpably guilty! The war tribunal excommunicated me from their society. I was eternally cast out.' Leirtod pauses then continues in a voice thick with loathing. 'Expulsion was bad enough but do you know what made me hate your father *even more*?'

Josh shakes his head then realises that Leirtod can't see his movement in the darkness. 'No,' he gulps.

'Lumaluce begged the war generals to reinstate me. He said ...' Leirtod can hardly bear to repeat the words. 'He said he *loved* me ...'

Joshua's whole body tingles with pride. Oh yes, his dad was a *legend* all right!

'His gift of love and forgiveness infuriated me. I wanted his death more than ever but as an outcast I would never be able to get near him. For centuries I waited to get my revenge on Lumaluce and then my chance came. Legends can travel back and forth in time and your father took a trip into the future where he took a mortal wife who bore him a son.'

'Tom!' cries Josh.

'Lumaluce's firstborn son is of no concern to me – he is not of legendary stock. Then you were conceived. From the second your heart ticked I knew you were your father reborn, and then I knew how I would revenge myself. I would make Lumaluce suffer by killing YOU!'

Desperate to prolong the conversation that literally has him on a knife edge, Josh quickly thinks of another question.

'Was it *you* who drowned my father in the Thames?'

'Oh, absolutely. I removed him from his incarnation as a mortal man and he joined the Immortals in the Fields of Joy. It was pleasant to see his mortal family thrown into chaos. Their agonised cries were sweet music to my ears,' he adds with vicious relish.

Uncontrollable fury boils up inside Joshua. His mother's sorrow at the loss of a beloved husband, Tom and himself left to grow up without a father – all because of a madman in a time warp. With a knife poised very close to him Josh knows he should stay quiet but he can't.

'How could you do that?' he blurts out.

'Very easily. It was an intense pleasure,' Leirtod replies in a sadistic voice. 'Such a pity that *you* didn't die as I'd hoped.'

Joshua recalls the stories of his premature birth and his first months hovering between life and death in an incubator in St Thomas's Hospital.

'Unfortunately you clung on to a thread of life and on your true birth date the Legends gave you their blessing and life surged through you.' Leirtod sighs regretfully. 'For ten years they protected you from evil – from me! But centuries of waiting had taught me patience. I knew I would have you in your eleventh year.' He lurches towards Joshua. 'Ahh! It's been a long wait!'

Feeling his hot rank breath on the left side of his neck, Josh hurls his body over to the right and rolls across the cell floor. He smashes into a wall where he stays curled up in the smallest ball possible. Unfortunately Muck squeaks in pain, alerting Leirtod to their whereabouts. He pounces on Joshua and grabs him around the throat.

'Now I've got you!' he hisses as he shakes the life out of the boy.

'Ghhh ...' he chokes as Leirtod's fingers close around his windpipe. 'Father, help me!'

Suddenly the cell door is flung wide open and a guard shines a light inside. Leirtod drops Joshua on to the floor and vanishes into the darkness.

'Here's a crazy man to keep you company!' yells the guard. 'I'll leave a light so that you two can introduce yourselves.'

Lying in a trembling heap on the ground Josh shades his eyes against the light, which momentarily blinds him. He sees a tall, skinny man with intense eyes that seem to bore into him. His clothes are dirty, his hair is long and he has bits of food in his straggly beard. Great, thinks Josh. I've lost a murderer only to have him replaced by a dirty tramp!

'I'm Pythagoras from Samos – do you eat beans?'

Josh shakes his head. 'No, but my mum serves up the best mushy peas south of the River Thames.'

'Peas, beans, peas, beans. They're all pulses,' rants the newcomer. 'Bad for you.'

'Why?'

'Wind! Very *very* anti-social. What's your name pea-eater?' he demands.

'I'm Joshua Cross from England.'

'Where's England?'

'South of Hyperborea.'

'Ah, so you're a barbarian!'

'No way – I'm British!'

'All foreigners are barbarians.'

'Why?'

'Because they babble, of course. Ba-ba-ba-ba! That's what they sound like – hence the word *barbarian*.'

Pythagoras hunkers down on the cell floor.

'I see you have a lyre. Entertain me with a song, silver-eyed barbarian.'

Josh doesn't feel like entertaining anybody but there is something so imperiously mad about this stranger that he thinks he ought to oblige. The only song he can sing all the way through is Jimi Hendrix's 'Wild Thing'. He holds up Apollo's lyre and says, 'You've got to imagine this is a guitar.'

'What's a guitar?'

'It's like a lyre but wired up to electricity. Oh, you won't know about that,' he remembers. 'Anyway, it sounds *very very* loud.'

Pythagoras nods and Josh starts to gyrate around the cell yelling, 'Wild Thing! Ding, ding, ding-a-ding-ding-ding! You make my heart sing! Ding, ding, ding-a-ding-ding-ding! You make e-v-e-r-y-t-h-i-n-g … grooooovy!' At the end he turns breathlessly to Pythagoras, who is not even mildly entertained by his efforts.

'Mmm, very discordant,' he says.

'Sorry, I never had singing lessons,' Josh replies.

'Now to pass the rest of the night away I will teach you a great mathematical secret,' says Pythagoras with tremendous excitement. 'One which is known only to my followers on the island of Croton.'

As the mad old man scrawls figures on the grimy prison floor, Joshua groans – the last thing he wants right now is a maths lesson.

'There we are,' announces Pythagoras. '$A^2 = B^2 + C^2$'

'HUH?'

'A-squared equals B-squared plus C-squared.'

'For all right-angled triangles, the square of the length of the longest side equals the squares of the lengths of the other two sides added together!' he rants.

Somewhere far back in Josh's brain a tiny bell tinkles. 'Hey, I've heard that before. It's the Hippopotamus's Nose theory.'

'Idiot! It's MY theory – *Pythagoras' Theorem*.'

Wildly gesticulating with his long bony arms, the old man starts to pace the cell.

'Perfect, precise, natural science!' he cries. 'It is all around us – perfect harmony of the perfect ratios. Mathematics is vital to our understanding of the world. How else can we understand our relationship with nature, music or the movement of the stars if we don't have the basic principles of mathematics?'

Josh feels deeply inadequate. Not for the first time he yearns for the presence of Dido. She'd be on the case with old Pythagoras, no fear. She'd be chatting about his theory and ratios and natural harmony. All he can do is sit in the half light with his chin on his chest.

'My friend Dido says maths is cool,' he says feebly.

'Cool? You mean cold?'

'No, I mean, er, interesting.'

'Oh, yes, little barbarian, mathematics is interesting.' Pythagoras smiles like a man possessed. 'Mathematics *is beautiful*!'

'Well, I wouldn't go that far!' mutters Josh under his breath.

As dawn breaks, their awesome conversation is brought to a close by Hermes popping through the cell window! Pythagoras looks only mildly surprised then asks the Immortal if he eats beans! Ignoring the mad old man, Hermes turns to Joshua.

'Zeus has threatened to fry me on the end of one of his thunderbolts if I don't get you and your mortal friend out of prison right away.'

Exhausted after a long hard night Joshua grumbles, 'You should never have left me alone in here in the first place – Leirtod nearly killed me!'

Hermes' eyes flash at him.

'You may be protected by Zeus but that doesn't mean to say you can push your luck with me, brat!'

But Josh does push his luck.

'Can you get my friend Pythagoras out too?' he asks.

'Oh, all right,' says the Messenger God. 'On condition you put in a good word for me when you meet Athene at the Parthenon.'

'I'll say you were the most *courteous* of the gods.'

Hermes raps Josh with his moly stick. 'I don't do courtesy!'

Hermes magicks the three prisoners out of their cells then urges Josh to get a move on. Joshua hugs Stav, who hurries off to Olympia with the healing ointments Theagenes is eagerly awaiting. Josh then says his farewells to Pythagoras, who bows and goes his way – back to his weird mathematical community on the Island of Croton, where beans are banned from the menu!

After the gloom of the prison Joshua is blinded by the blazing-white heat of the morning. Hermes gives him an impatient shove.

'Come along, the goddess Athene is not one to be kept waiting.'

'I wouldn't be late if you hadn't abandoned me,' Joshua grumbles as he hurries after the Winged Messenger.

'Were you a snail in your former life?' Hermes demands impatiently.

'Zeus didn't bless me with wings on my feet, like you!'

Fortunately a group of street vendors hurry towards them and Hermes fades away. Left alone Joshua is able to admire the classical white temples towering high over the city. On one of the hilltops, overlooking the placid aquamarine sea, is a gigantic statue of a god holding a raised sword which shimmers in the golden heat haze.

'That's Athene's statue on the Acropolis,' Hermes says as he pops up beside him. 'The Athenians think only the loftiest site is worthy of their patron goddess. They built a splendid temple too – it's called the Parthenon. Get a move on and I'll show you around.'

Hermes leads him up the hill to the Acropolis then takes him into the Parthenon. Joshua gazes at the sculptured marble frieze around the wall and realises with a shock that he's seen these carved charioteers and prancing Arab horses in the British Museum in London! Only a few weeks ago Fingers had taken the class on a school trip. Nobody was in the slightest bit interested in ancient history until they saw the Elgin Marbles. Dido had been knocked out by the racing horses and Steve had been blown away by the Greek charioteers. Josh wished that his friends could be beside him now, not just *seeing* the marbles so new and fresh but able to *feel* the cool stone of the Parthenon under their fingertips.

'I've seen these carvings in London,' he tells Hermes. 'They're the Elgin Marbles!'

'Don't be foolish!' snaps Hermes. 'They were carved by

132

Pheidias to commemorate the Great Panathenaia, a procession that's held every year to honour Athene. They belong here on the Acropolis – they're *GREEK*,' he says stressing the word.

'So how come they're in the British Museum?' Josh asks and then the penny drops. Somewhere down the centuries somebody must have *stolen* them from the Parthenon! Maybe it'd been the guy Elgin himself who'd removed them from Greece and shipped them back to London. What a cheek!

Hermes gives Josh a sharp nudge in the ribs and turns him towards a towering statue of Athene. As he bows low he realises he has come empty-handed to her altar – he has nothing to sacrifice to the goddess! He feels Muck wriggle in his pouch, the pup is all he's got but he can't sacrifice his dog! Suddenly a basket of white doves is dumped down on the ground in front of him.

'Can't you remember *anything*?' Hermes hisses furiously in his ear.

A soft voice sings out from behind Athene's towering statue.

'Joshua Cross – Lumaluce is impatient to see you.'

Though he's completely overwhelmed by the nearness of the goddess Joshua manages to reply.

'I long to see my father but my journey keeps, er, taking me to funny places!'

'You have had friends to guide you. All have given you gifts that bring you ever closer to Lumaluce.'

Joshua bows his head. 'I am grateful to all of them.'

Standing in homage before Athene he recalls those who have helped him. Beginning way back with Tiresias, who set him off on his quest with the purse of white barley and a coin for Charon the Ferryman, then Mate, who gave him directions. And what was the first thing Stav had done? Given him a sausage butty then helped him jump ship! On board the *Dolphin* he met Heracles, who not only protected him from Leirtod but also gave him information on how to find the Underworld. Apollo gave him a lyre to charm Charon and Cerberus. Pythagoras had *tried* to teach him maths; even grumpy Hermes had given him the gift of protection. Without his guides and their gifts he would never have reached Athene's high altar in the Parthenon. He would still be hanging around Zachynthus harbour waiting for a boat or, worse still, have been trampled to death under the flying hooves of Hippodrax.

The goddess interrupts his deep thoughts.

'Mortal boy, My gift to you is wisdom.'

'Wisdom! But I'm not clever, goddess.'

'Wisdom is not a mark of intelligence. It is an ability to think your way *around* a problem.'

'*How* do you do that?'

'By using your natural wit. Believe me, it *is* there,' she assures him.

A thousand questions burst to his lips but Athene stops him.

'You began this journey by knowing *nothing* of your

father. You will end it by knowing him well. *If* you outwit Leirtod you too will enter the realm of legends and join your father in history.'

'Do I have to die first?' he blurts out.

'You might die if you do not use the gift of wisdom that I am about to bestow on you,' the goddess replies. 'Continue your quest, Joshua Cross. I will not walk with you as Heracles and Hermes did, but you will feel my presence.'

Joshua bows low to the goddess, who adds, 'Before you leave the city you will meet the wisest man in the world. Hearken to his words – he too has something of value to give you.'

As Josh turns to walk away he bumps into the white doves crammed into the wicker basket.

'Slit their throats outside the Parthenon,' whispers Hermes in his ear.

'I can't kill an animal!'

Hermes groans in frustration. 'You are such a mortal weed! Ask a priest to perform the sacrifice for you.'

Joshua is grateful that he doesn't have to kill the pretty birds who flutter and squawk in the priest's hands. With practised ease he slits their throats and lets their blood flow over the sacred stone.

'It is auspicious,' says the priest as he examines the entrails.

'What does that mean?' asks Josh.

'The goddess is pleased with your sacrifice,' Hermes

explains.

'That's a relief. I wouldn't want to sacrifice another batch of doves!'

'Well, I have concluded my errand,' says Hermes with immense relief. 'Now I can return to the pleasures of Mount Olympus,' he adds with undisguised glee.

Josh smiles at the mischievous god. 'I shall miss you, Winged Messenger.'

'I *shan't* miss you!' Hermes replies. 'Though you have improved a little along the way,' he adds grudgingly. 'Watch out for Leirtod. He will be waiting for you at every corner!'

With these comforting words the Winged Messenger is gone, and Josh is again alone in Ancient Greece.

CHAPTER TWELVE

Sappho

As Josh takes his last look at the dazzling Acropolis he hears a familiar flutter of wings and Mate flies down and lands on his shoulder.

'Good job you weren't around five minutes ago,' he chuckles. 'You might have gone the same way as the sacrificial doves!'

Mate squawks indignantly and Muck scrambles out of her pouch yapping excitedly. The seagull quickly pops a piece of meat into her mouth, which the pup chews then ravenously yaps for more.

'I'd better find her some food,' says Josh then remembers that he hasn't got any money. He hadn't needed any with Stav and Heracles around but now he's flat broke with a starving pup to feed! Mate screeches and flies off, giving Josh the now familiar backward glance which seems to mean 'Watch this space – I'll be back.'

Josh walks through the city and finds some stale bread under a bakery stall. He breaks it up into crumbs and offers it to Muck, who looks deeply disappointed.

'It's that or fresh air,' he tells her firmly.

As Muck chomps the hard crusts Joshua wanders into a wide sunny square where he sees two big boys chasing after a girl with waist-length, flowing red hair. The biggest boy grabs her by the hair and shakes her like a dog.

'Ahhh!' she screams in agony.

'What have you got in your hand, little scribbler?' he sneers.

The other boy snatches a papyrus scroll from the girl's hands and waves it mockingly in front of her face.

'NO! Give it back!' she begs.

The boy unrolls the scroll and starts to read from it.

'A poem by Sappho!' he laughs. 'Listen to this load of camel dung!' Striking a silly girlie pose he reads what's she's written.

'A girl whose hair is wreathed in garlands of fresh flowers,
'Sits with the sun on her face in an Arcadian bower.'

Both boys look at each other and go, 'OOOOOH!' then start to tug her hair again.

'You're a stupid girl! You should be at home with the women, working in the kitchen – cooking food for men like us!' yells the biggest boy.

'Yeah, women don't write,' taunts the other.

'You're jealous!' she cries in fury. 'Jealous because I'm cleverer than you!'

The boys are enraged by her stinging insult.

'We are superior to you, girl,' says the big lout. 'We fight, we govern, we command—'

'But you don't *think*!' she says. 'You don't wonder about

138

life and how you could change things.'

'We don't want to change things – we like things just the way they are. We're male and we're superior!' announces the biggest boy.

To prove it he rips her papyrus scroll into fragments, then laughing at the top of his voice he swaggers off with his friend.

Josh hurries over to help the weeping girl pick up the pieces.

'What do you want?' she asks sharply.

'I thought you might need a hand.'

'I don't want your help.'

Joshua ignores her bad manners and carries on helping her. 'Those boys were pretty nasty.'

'ALL boys are nasty.'

'I'm not,' he says in his own defence.

'Why should you be different? All boys grow up thinking they are gods. Girls are little better than slaves.'

'You'd get locked up if you said sexist things like that in my country.'

The girl looks at him in amazement. 'Do you come from Thrace?' she asks. 'I've heard the Thracians treat their women better than the Greeks.'

'I come from the far north. A cold, grey country near Hyperborea.'

'And how do northern men treat their female citizens?'

'Boys and girls are treated the same – it's against the law to discriminate.'

The girl's eyes widen. They're dazzlingly blue, just like Dido's. 'You mean I could go to school and write poems *all day* and walk about on my own and not be sold off in marriage as soon as I'm old enough to bear children?' she asks incredulously.

'Sure,' he nods. 'What happens here in Ancient Greece?'

'If you have the misfortune to be born female, *nothing*. When you're born you may be left in a pot to die in the street. If your parents decide to keep you then you will be brought up in the household, where, if you're lucky, a slave might teach you to read – that's if you've got a slave with half a brain! At fifteen your toys are taken from you and you are married off to whoever your father pleases, usually the fattest, ugliest but richest man in the area. As a bride you are removed from all that is familiar and taken into another household where you will bear children. If you have too many daughters then your husband will put the female baby into a pot and take it out into the street where it may die. Thus the cycle begins all over again, and as a female I have no power and no right to fight against it.' Her blue eyes flash with fury. 'Can you begin to understand what it's like to be born free but to be treated like a slave until your death?'

Joshua is at a loss for words.

'Women in my country are very important. My friend Dido, who looks a bit like you, is the cleverest person I know. She writes poems and plays and never stops reading books. You'd really like her.'

'Your country sounds like heaven! Take me there?' begs Sappho.

Joshua shuffles uncomfortably.

'That could be tricky,' he mutters. 'Anyway I'm not exactly sure when I'm going back.'

'Are you a slave?'

'No. I'm here for a short time, like a holiday,' he adds vaguely.

She holds out her hand in gesture of friendship. 'I'm Sappho. What's your name?'

'Joshua Cross.'

'Are you hungry?'

'Starving!'

'Come with me.'

Sappho takes him to a large single-storey house which has a courtyard open to the sky. The walls of the courtyard are decorated with pretty pebble mosaics and in its centre is a shallow pool. The minute they enter the house a man's voice thunders out.

'SAPPHO!'

The girl jumps and quickly pushes Joshua in front of her. 'It's my father,' she whispers nervously.

A thick-set man wearing a short white tunic bears down on them with a scowl on his face.

'How many times do I have to tell you to stay in the house with the women?'

He raises his hand to hit Sappho but she blurts out, 'I went out with the slave to buy food.'

Her father's hand freezes in mid-air as he stares at Joshua.

'What's your name, slave?' he demands.

Too scared to speak Joshua looks at Sappho.

'Lost your tongue?' snaps the grumpy father.

'His name is Ajax. He's from Hyperborea.'

'Hyperborea!' her father exclaims in disgust. 'That rain-drenched dump at the end of the world. Well stop hanging around here doing nothing – go and tidy the library, boy.'

As Sappho leads him through the men's part of the house, which is called the *andron*, Joshua asks, 'Why did you tell your dad I'm a slave? He'll think he owns me and I've got things to do – people to see.'

'You can always run away,' she says.

'Don't slaves have their hands chopped off for trying to escape?'

'No, that's the punishment for stealing. Slaves are beheaded if they attempt to escape.'

'Oh, that really cheers me up!' says Josh. 'And why did you give me a stupid name like Ajax? I sound like a cleaning powder!'

'I thought you'd be safer with a false identity.'

'You could have given me a good name, like Heracles or Perseus,' he grumbles.

'You're not handsome enough to be named after a superhero!'

The library is a big room with low tables, stools, and wooden chests overflowing with papyrus scrolls.

'My father is an ignorant pig!' Sappho announces. 'He can hardly add up, never mind read. But my great great great grandmother was Sappho the poet. That's why I love reading and writing – I'm just like her!' She runs excitedly from chest to chest, pulling out scrolls. 'Homer, Euripides, Aristophanes, Sophocles ... plays, poems, history, philosophy – they're all here. Oh, I love them!' she raves as she unrolls one of the hundreds of scrolls.

'What am I supposed to do while you've got your nose buried in a scroll?'

'You can pretend to be tidying up.'

'Great, I thought you invited me back here for something to eat,' he reminds her.

'Later ... later,' she mutters as she immerses herself in her reading. 'Won't you get into trouble for being alone with a BOY?' he teases.

She shrugs. 'Slaves are not a problem. They're subhuman.'

Joshua is genuinely shocked by her callousness.

'How can you be such a fighter for women's right and ignore the fact that you keep people in your house who have no human rights at all?'

'Slaves don't have real feelings like we do.'

'Yes they do!'

Their argument stops as the heavy wooden door is flung open and Sappho's father strides into the library.

'This room stinks!' he bellows as he kicks over a couple of wooden chests in disgust. 'Read some of this rubbish to me, Hyperborean.'

Sappho shoves the scroll she's holding into his hand.

'Er …' Joshua dithers. 'This is a play called Lysistrata written by Aristophanes.'

'Yes, yes, get on with it,' barks Sappho's father irritably.

Joshua starts. 'It is not easy for a woman to get out and about. She has to look after her husband, make sure the servant girl does her work, tuck the baby up in bed, wash it, feed it—'

'Quite right!' exclaims the father as he frowns at his daughter. 'It is more profitable to have a cow in calf than a daughter who cannot even carry on the family name.'

Sappho's brilliant eyes blaze with fury. 'Everyone wants to raise a son, nobody wants a daughter.'

Joshua decides to break the tense atmosphere by reading from another scroll.

'This is written by Sophocles, would you like to hear it, lord?'

Sappho's father yawns. Josh takes that as a yes and reads.

'Often I have thought what it is to be a woman and realised we are nothing. When we are girls our lives are sweet and pleasant, but once we grow up we have to leave and become something to be bought or sold.'

Joshua stops and looks nervously from father to daughter. Instead of easing the tension he's heightened it.

144

'Sophocles sympathises with the inferior status of women more than my own family,' Sappho cries out.

Her father crosses the room and grabs her by the shoulders.

'Oww! You're hurting me,' she protests.

'I'll break every bone in your body if you answer me back, girl!,' he snarls and throwing her aside he storms out of the room.

Surrounded by the scrolls on which her great grand-mother wrote her poetry, Sappho sinks to the ground and weeps. 'Oh, if only I had been born a boy.'

'Why don't you run away?' Joshua asks.

She raises her tear-stained face and looks at him as if he were a madman. 'Where would I go? Who would have me?'

Joshua can see her Ancient Greek point of view – she can go nowhere. His heart aches for the girl with so much passion for life stifled inside her.

'It really will be good for women in the future,' Josh blurts out.

'Then my daughters will enjoy it,' she whispers sadly.

'You could easily be an ancestor of my best friend Dido. Believe me, Sappho, she's *really* enjoying her life!'

They leave the library and go to the kitchen, which is in the *gynakeion*, the women's quarter.

'Men aren't allowed in here,' Sappho tells him.

'So where do they eat?' he asks in bewilderment.

'They don't eat with women – they eat in the dining room in the andron.'

'Do I have to eat with your grumpy dad?' he asks nervously.

She giggles, clearly amused at the idea. 'My father wouldn't sit down to eat with a slave. You have to eat outside – with the dogs.'

Josh shakes his head in disbelief.

'Man! You Ancient Greeks really know how to make a traveller feel welcome.'

While Sappho searches for food, Josh and Muck wait in the courtyard outside the kitchen.

'Shhsh!' Josh says as the pup whines impatiently for her supper. Suddenly his heart misses a beat as the ground beneath his feet starts to shake. Surely it can't be Hippodrax? He wouldn't dare to enter a house packed with people, would he? When he hears a shrill neighing rapidly followed by the sound of thundering hooves, Josh knows that the centaur is upon him!

Clutching Muck he crouches behind the well, praying that the monster will pass him by, but Hippodrax has smelt him! The pounding hooves stop, to be replaced by a slow, purposeful clip-clop as the centaur tracks him down. As Joshua stares into Hippodrax's mad topaz-yellow eyes he prays like he's never prayed before.

'Oh, Athene, *please* help me!'

'Think, Joshua,' her voice sings back. '*Think ...*'

'I'm in no position to think!'

The centaur bends his head and starts to butt his chest. Josh's terror is suddenly surpassed by a grim determination to live. Screaming in angry defiance he grabs Hippodrax's enormous hairy ears and twists them as hard as he can. The centaur grunts in pain and tries to toss his head but Joshua grips his smelly ears even harder. Squealing in anger the centaur bucks then rears up and tries to grasp Joshua around the neck. Josh doesn't relax his grip even though the muscles in his arms feel like they're going to explode under the pressure. Gathering the last of his strength he twists the beast's head to the right, sending him momentarily off balance. In that vital split second Joshua leaps to freedom and starts to run! Unfortunately his struggle with the centaur has taken him some distance from the house. How can he possibly outrun the beast who is hard on his heels? Where can he hide from Hippodrax? Suddenly he spots a big old oak tree at the edge of the kitchen courtyard, which he hurls himself into. Laughing in triumph Josh gazes down at the centaur, who's headbutting the tree.

'Go on, ugly mug!' he goads. 'Bash your brains out!'

Hippodrax's frenzied headbanging is interrupted by Sappho calling from the kitchen courtyard.

'Joshua! Joshua!'

Her timely arrival sends the centaur galloping back to his master to report yet another failed mission. Limp with relief Joshua slowly climbs down from the oak tree.

'I told you to wait in the courtyard,' Sappho says crossly.

Too weak to go into details he simply says, 'Sorry, I fancied a run!'

'I've got you and the dog a bit of barley bread,' she says, handing him a crust. 'I didn't want to arouse the slaves' curiosity by taking more.'

Joshua gives some crumbs to Muck then wolfs down the bread, which lands in his empty stomach, making him feel hungrier than ever.

'Come back to the library,' she urges.

Fearful of Hippodrax's return with his demonic master, Joshua is impatient to be gone.

'I've got to go. Don't tell your dad I've run away,' he adds quickly. 'I don't want to be dragged back here for a ceremonial decapitation!'

As he turns to leave, his path is blocked by a plump woman who screams furiously at Sappho.

'Daughter! How many times have you been told not to talk to strange males?'

'He's a traveller, mother,' Sappho quickly tells her.

The word 'traveller' has a magical effect on the irate mother. In a flash her manner changes. 'A traveller!' she exclaims. 'Then you are welcome to my house.'

Joshua smiles in relief. 'Thank you.'

'We Greeks have an ancient rule of hospitality. It is our custom to offer food and drink to our visitors, who in turn must extend a welcome to travellers in their own country.'

'My mum always extends a warm welcome to *every-*

body!' says Joshua, vividly recalling the endless foreigners queuing up outside Shakespeare's Chippy eager for a bag of Mrs Cross's steaming hot fish and chips.

'Then you are welcome in my house,' says the woman graciously.

Joshua turns to Sappho and whispers, 'This is a different reception to the one your mean old man gave me!'

Sappho's mum takes him into the kitchen where a fire burns in the middle of the clay floor. She points to the large pots bubbling over the glowing embers. 'There's cutlet of eel, squid, boiled pigs' trotters, black pudding, and wild thrush stewed in honey.'

Josh recoils at the menu but Muck is so hungry she nearly nose-dives into the pot of pigs' trotters! Hungry as he is, Josh cautiously asks for *a bit* of everything.

'Fill up his plate,' Sappho's mother commands the slaves, who usher him towards a divan where they position him in an awkward semi-reclining position. Josh whispers to Sappho who is watching him with some amusement.

'I can't eat here, with the women! Shouldn't I go into the andron with the men?'

She giggles and props two big pillows behind his back. 'You're not *really* a man!' she teases.

'Is that supposed to make me feel better or worse?' he asks.

'Relax and enjoy your meal.'

149

'Can't you sit on the couch and eat with me?' he implores.

'No! Females never eat with male guests.'

'Then stay near – I haven't a clue what I'm doing.'

A servant girl presents him with a drinking cup, which she fills with a mixture of sweet wine and water. Josh raises it to his lips and is just about to take a big gulp when Sappho stops him.

'You must pour the first few drops on to the ground as an offering to the gods,' she tells him. Thinking of Athene's huge generosity, Joshua pours half of his cup on to the hard clay floor then thirstily swallows the rest.

Another servant appears with his plate of food, which he has to eat with his fingers, using hot barley bread to soak up the juices. It is so delicious he can hardly bear the thought of sharing it with Muck, but he has no choice. Smelling the food she scrambles out of her pouch and devours the eel and squid cooked in a tangy mixture of oil, lemon, garlic and fresh herbs. Joshua gorges on the sweet honeyed flesh from the thrush's tiny carcass.

'Mmm! I could eat ten of those!' he tells Sappho, but the thought of scoffing ten little songbirds immediately brings on a rush of twenty-first-century guilt. 'Well, maybe five!' he compromises.

The songbirds are followed by goat's cheese, figs, and crispy pastries crammed with a delicious mixture of nuts and honey. Stuffed with good things Joshua flops back on the couch more relaxed than he's been since he first set foot in the land of the Ancient Greeks. His peace is shattered by an angry cry that rings through the gynakeion.

'WIFE! Where is my food?'

'My father!' gasps Sappho.

Her terrified mother runs to the kitchen, where she hits the trembling slaves with a stick.

'Take the food to your master!' she screams.

In the noise and bustle Sappho hurries Joshua out of the house and leads him through a network of narrow streets back into the centre of the city.

'The agora is that way,' she says, pointing directly ahead.

'What's an agora?'

'The main square, it's down there,' she tells him hurriedly. 'I must return. If my father finds me missing again, he will beat me and lock me up with the animals.'

Joshua's heart aches for this lively girl who is so like Dido. 'I wish I could take you with me.'

'This is my life. Pray that I will be given greater freedom in another destiny.'

He smiles knowingly. 'Sappho, believe me, *I know you will!*'

She extends her hand in farewell. 'It has been good to meet you, Joshua Cross. May all the gods go with you.'

He shakes her hand and smiles into her dazzling blue eyes. 'Farewell, Sappho – keep up with the writing!'

CHAPTER THIRTEEN

Splitting Hairs with Socrates

As Joshua hurries towards the agora, his thoughts are full of Sappho. Is her father beating her or her mother – or both – for failing to produce his meal on time? For sure, the slaves will be getting a good thrashing – after all they are sub-human by Ancient Greek standards! Lost in thought, he hardly notices the singing in his head, then he realises it is Athene speaking to him.

'Forget about Sappho.'

'Goddess, forgive me!' he whispers. 'I can't!'

'I understand what women endure. Trust me, all things will change.'

'Can't you change it *now* for Sappho,' he implores.

'Her time will come, Joshua. Meanwhile you have a journey to make if you are to see your father.'

'I want to see him but I don't where to find a boat that's going to the Ionian Sea!'

'Good. You remember your destination.'

'How could I forget? I have to board a ship that will

take me to Sicily where the River of Lamentation and the River of Flaming Fire converge.'

'Make your way to Piraeus harbour, outside the city walls,' Athene replies, then her voice fades away like music.

Joshua quickens his pace. 'I don't want to be like Odysseus and spend the next ten years roaming the seas of the Ancient World,' he tells Muck, who's popped up for a breath of fresh air. 'I want see my dad then return to the future where there are supermarkets, tellies, computers, video games, trainers – and best of all, my mum's chips!'

Chattering to the pup, he wanders into the agora that Sappho mentioned. His progress is hampered by a noisy crowd who are standing listening to an old man in a long, white tunic trimmed with a green and purple border. He addresses the crowd in a loud, commanding voice.

'All experiences aren't truly real – whatever we sense might not be the real thing.'

Joshua stops dead in his tracks. How many times on his journey through Ancient Greece has he wondered if he was living the real thing or just dreaming? He elbows his way through the crowd and stands on his tiptoes to get a glimpse of the person who's talking. He sees an amazingly ugly and very short man who again startles him with his words.

'What you see around you is an illusion.'

'Socrates!' an old woman calls from the crowd, 'You're a philosopher – the wisest man in the world. WHY do you speak in riddles?'

So *this* is the wisest man in the world Athene told him

to look out for. Joshua wriggles to the front and sees Socrates holding a red apple up to the crowd.

'How do we know that we are all seeing the same red on this apple?'

'Because we've got eyes and we can see that the apple is red,' somebody shouts out.

'Ah-ha, not so!' declares Socrates. 'We *believe* we're seeing the same colour.'

'That's donkey dung!' mocks an old man with no teeth.

Clearly enjoying the challenge, Socrates smiles.

'Fetch me three bowls of water and I'll show you how our senses can deceive us.'

Several eager kids hurry forwards and place three bowls of water in a straight line on the ground before Socrates. He points to the bowl on the left.

'This contains hot water,' he announces. 'The bowl on the right contains cold water, and the one in the middle has a mixture of the two. It's luke-warm.'

He then turns to the toothless old man and asks him to put his hand in the bowl on the left.

'Oooh! It's hot,' yelps the man as he hops up and down, making the crowd laugh.

'Now try putting your hand in the bowl on the right,' says Socrates.

'Brrr! That's cold,' says the old man as he shivers dramatically before the roaring crowd.

'Now put *both hands* in the middle bowl.'

The old man plunges his hands into the water in the

middle bowl and rolls his eyes in surprise.

'Great balls of fire! My left hand feels cold and yet my right hand feels hot. I don't understand – it's the same water.'

The crowd surge forward, trying to see if Socrates is tricking them by switching the bowls. He smiles in delight as he rams his point home to them.

'Often, how we experience the world is based on beliefs, rather than true knowledge. Your left hand is telling you that the water is cold. Your right believes it to be hot. Both are in a sense true.'

The old man takes his hands out of the bowl and waves them in.

'My hands are telling the truth!' he jokes.

'True opinions are a fine thing but they run away from a man's mind until they are tethered by him working out the reason *why* they're true. Remember my words: it is hard to define reality.'

Joshua is *riveted*! He waits for the crowd to disperse, then approaches the wisest man in the world, who is irritably ticking off a young man beside him.

'Plato, how many times do I have to tell you? It is NOT necessary to write down *everything* I say in my philosophical dialogues.'

'If your arguments are not written down, how else will they be remembered?'

'Plato, people *listen* to what I say and discuss it, which is *exactly* what I want them to do. My philosophies are based on the oral tradition – I'm not interested in scribbling down every detail on a bit of papyrus that might blow away in the wind!'

'But I admire what you say – I *want* to record it,' insists Plato.

'Well, don't do it near me, it really puts me off my flow!' grumbles Socrates.

Josh coughs politely.

'Sorry to interrupt your discussion.'

'It's not a discussion – it's a *row*!' barks Socrates. He stops when he notices the boy's colouring. 'Zeus! You have eyes the colour of olive trees and hair like milk! Where are you from, boy?'

'South of Hyperborea,' Josh replies.

'Are you a slave?'

'No, I'm a traveller in time.'

'Ah-ha!' Socrates smiles and turns to Plato, 'A philosopher in the making!'

Plato nods and gives his papyrus pen a good lick. He's clearly all set to record whatever words might fall from his master's lips.

'What is time?' asks Socrates.

'That's exactly the question I want to ask you,' Josh replies, 'You see, I've been dipping in and out of time quite a lot recently, and I wonder if you could run that "what is reality?" thing past me one more time?'

Socrates throws an arm around Josh's shoulder and sets off at a slow stroll around the agora, followed by Plato, who's desperately trying to walk, write and listen!

'The first thing to remember is this – we are all in flux.'

'With respect, sir, I've got a strong feeling I might be more in flux than most!'

'As you heard, genuine knowledge cannot be obtained from what is around us because our senses deceive us.'

'You mean I'm *imagining* everything I see?'

'An interesting question, boy – one which my friend Plato and I often discuss.'

Socrates stops when he sees Joshua's puzzled expression.

'Let me tell you a story,' he says as he starts to walk on again.

'Once upon a time, there were a group of prisoners deep in the bottom of a cave where they had been since their birth. They were kept chained up, facing a wall, and *never* allowed to turn and see what was behind them. The prisoners had spent their entire lives looking only at the shadows on the wall. Then one day, one of the prisoners – let's call him Alexis – is released from his chains and told he's free. For the first time in his life he can look around, but when he turns he is blinded by a brilliant light. After a while his eyes adjust and he sees that the light is in fact a fire burning. Between the fire and the prisoners is a path that is used by the jailers, who walk along it carrying objects which cast shadows on to the wall in front of the prisoners. Alexis suddenly realises that he has *never* seen a real object before. When he was a prisoner, he saw only the shadows of the objects, cast on to the wall in front of him. Like all the other prisoners, he believed that these shadows actually *were* the real objects. He mistook what he saw on the wall for reality.'

Plato interrupts. 'Was your last line, *He mistook what he saw on the wall for reality?*'

'YES!' snaps Socrates.

'Brilliant – couldn't have put it better myself.'

Socrates ignores Plato's enthusiastic comment and continues his story.

'Alexis now understands that what he had earlier taken to be the real world was merely a parade of shadows. He and all the other prisoners have been fooled – the real world was hidden from them. The jailers lead Alexis outside, where he sees the beauty of the world for the first time. He feels sorry that the prisoners he's left behind won't ever know about the wonders he's seen and decides to return to them. Down in the depths of the cave he stumbles and bumps into things in the darkness causing the prisoners to think that his journey has made him blind! When Alexis tells them about the real world outside, they turn away from him and engross themselves, watching the shadows on the wall in front of them.

'"Leave us alone!" they say.

'"Listen to me," Alexis begs.

'"GO AWAY!" they shout.'

Joshua bursts out laughing.

"That's exactly what my brother says when I try and talk to him during Eastenders!'

'What's Eastenders?' Socrates asks.

'It's a story, but lots of people think it's real, just like your prisoners thought the shadows on the wall were real.'

'They are deluding themselves,' says Socrates solemnly.

'I'll tell my brother he's deluding himself the next time I see him!' chuckles Josh. 'Please go on with your story – what happens to Alexis?'

'He tells the prisoners that they're merely watching shadows, which sends them into a fury. They hurl rocks at him and drive him away.

'"We know what's real and what's not!" they cry.

'With blood dripping from his wounds, Alexis leaves his friends and family down in the cave, to waste away their lives watching shadows. They *never do* find out the truth.'

Socrates' eyes bore into Josh's.

'Have you any idea what I'm talking about, young Hyperborean?'

'Yes, you've taught me that I can't just take everything on face value and accept things that people say are *the truth*. I must work out for myself whether in fact they are true.'

Plato gives him a nudge with his elbow. 'Would you mind if I quoted you on that line?'

Joshua blushes. 'I'm no philosopher!'

'Oh, you could be,' Plato assures him.

'But stick to the *oral* tradition, boy,' Socrates insists, 'Don't go scribbling every word down on bits of papyrus like *somebody* I know!' he says as he gives Plato a dirty look.

Joshua decides it's time to leave, before he gets caught up in another Socrates-v-Plato philosophical argy-bargy.

'Thank you,' he says.

Socrates raises a hand in blessing.

'The Gods go with you in your quest for truth.'

'I'll remember your wise words,' says Joshua.

'You won't have to,' chuckles Socrates as he turns to Plato who's scribbling furiously. 'My friend here has written them all down – you'll be able to read them any time you want!'

Josh leaves Athens deep in thought. In the future he was an academic dummy, useless at everything but football, yet here he can speak and understand Ancient Greek as if it were his mother tongue. He can discuss maths and philosophy and he's a mine of information on the Greek myths and legends! Did his father endow him with these gifts to help him on his journey? Or is it Athene's wisdom kicking in?

Not heeding where his feet are taking him, Josh is surprised to find himself standing at one of the city gates on the outskirts of Athens. He looks from left to right and mutters:

'Eeeny, meeny, miny, mo – which way to Piraeus?'

'AWWWK!'

'MATE!'

Josh looks up and sees the big seagull circling the air above him. The bird dips his right wing, as if indicating, then swerves off to the right.

'I guess that's the way we're going, Muck!'

The pup scrambles out of his pouch and wriggles into the crook of Joshua's arm as he hurries after the seagull. Suddenly a flame of gold blazes out from Athene's towering statue on the Acropolis. Josh shades his eyes and sees her raised sword and the sun sparkling on her war helmet, then he hears her voice.

'Be *wise*, Joshua Cross.'

As her words ring loud inside his head, Joshua raises his hand in salute.

'I will not waste your gift, goddess.'

The sun moves on and the light is gone. Mate gives an impatient squawk and Josh breaks into a jog to keep up with him.

'What's the hurry?' he splutters as he pants along, with Muck bouncing in his arms. 'It's not like we've got a bus to catch!'

CHAPTER FOURTEEN

Wisdom Works Wonders!

An hour later Josh arrives in the ancient port of Piraeus, which is bristling with masted boats of all shapes and sizes. Most of them have bright-blue eyes painted on their prows, which Stavros told him were to ward off evil and help them navigate a safe course. As he makes his way towards the harbour, Josh sees a statue of a god holding a trident. He immediately recognises it as Poseidon, the Sea God. He remembers Heracles telling him that Poseidon rules the oceans, which he churns up when he's in a bad mood. Heracles said that Poseidon was *often* in a bad mood because he was often in a rage with somebody, be it man or god!

Josh stops at the water's edge and gazes at the boats bobbing on the gentle waves. Their watchful eyes seem to gaze back at him as he stands wondering which one he should try to board. All around he can hear sailors speaking many languages – Egyptian, Arabic, Syrian, Greek, Turkish, Italian. Each part of the Mediterranean seems to be represented here in the harbour of Piraeus. The only tongue he can't hear is his own!

Josh starts at a familiar screech. There are seagulls everywhere but he locates Mate perched on the mast of a ship. He has no doubt that this is the boat he's got to board. His heart beats nervously. It was terrifying jumping ship with Stavros leading the way – the thought of doing it on his own scares him to death! He approaches the boat, where two bronzed, swarthy sailors are swabbing the decks. He listens closely, trying to recognise the language they are speaking. Suddenly he realises they're speaking a sort of Italian. Then the penny drops – they're speaking LATIN! If they're Italian they might be heading home, or they could be on an outward journey to Turkey and the Middle East. Whether they're going east or west, Mate's made it crystal clear that *this* is the boat he's got to take.

Josh decides that hanging around on the wharf gawping at the boat he's planning to board illegally is not a wise move! He hurries away but is stopped in his tracks by Mate, who swoops down and lands on his shoulder. Josh feels something metallic slither down his back and land with a tinkle on the ground at his feet. It's a coin, a pretty coin in fact, with Athene's head on one side and the owl, her symbol, on the other side.

'MONEY!' he gasps. Then he looks up at Mate, who cocks his head cutely to one side. 'You little tea leaf,' laughs Josh, 'You thief – I bet you nicked this!'

As Mate flies up with a proud screech, Josh hurries back to the Latin sailors. The gods have blessed him with fluency in Ancient Greek but his language skills go no further than that. When it comes to Latin he's got to busk it! Waving his arms he indicates that he wants to sail with them and offers them his coin. One of the sailors takes it, bites it hard, then nods in approval. Through signs, gestures and pidgin Latin, they communicate.

'We go to Ionian Sea,' they tell him.

'When?' asks Josh.

Laughing, the sailors flap the sail and indicate they'll set off as soon as the wind gets up. Josh nods and they beckon him aboard where they feed him grilled salty fish, which Josh realises is sardines. Twenty-first-century tinned sardines never tasted this good! Smelling food, Muck pops up from her pouch and barks hungrily.

'Canis!' laughs one of the sailors in surprise.

He points to Josh.

'Et tu?'

Joshua assumes that they want to know his name.

'Joshua Cross. Tu?'

'Caecilius.'

He turns to the other one.

'And tu?'

'Julius.'

'Salve!' the sailors say.

Josh beams.

'Hi!'

The ship sets sail and Poseidon quickly hits the Mediterranean with a storm that sends the craft dipping and swirling over the raging waves. Down in the hold, Joshua believes he is dying. Never in his life has he felt so sick, or been so sick! He feels like he's been throwing up for hours. There's nothing in his stomach but he still keeps retching. He can't believe Caecilius and Julius can stay upright and keep the ship afloat. He curls up on a filthy old sack and sinks into a deep, dream-filled sleep.

He wakes up to the clatter of hooves and a shrill neighing.

The sound gives him such a fright he leaps to his feet just in time to avoid the flaying hooves of Hippodrax! The beast is back and intent on kicking his head in! Enraged, Hippodrax swings around and gives Joshua a thump in the guts.

'Ahhh!'

Winded, he drops to his knees then feels a searing stab in his back as Hippodrax's head butts him. A blood-red mist of pain swims before his eyes.

'Oh, Athene! *Why* didn't you give me strength as well as wisdom?'

As Hippodrax rears in triumph, Heracles' words echo in his head.

'Look into the face of your enemy!'

'I *am* looking. It is ugly and hairy and coming straight at me!'

'Fight your enemy!'

Josh lurches to his feet and stands square before Hippodrax, who paws the ground. Then with a high squeal he charges. With sweat breaking out all over his body, Josh doesn't move an inch. He waits until the beast is within hitting distance, then he steps quickly out of his flight-path. Hippodrax tries to put the breaks on, but he's going too fast and thunders into the wall, which he hits head-on. Slightly dazed, the raging beast turns on Joshua, who darts forward and springs on to his shoulders. Hippodrax is furious but the headlock Josh applies completely immobilises him. Grunting angrily he gallops around, chucking his head backwards in a wild attempt to throw Joshua off balance, but the boy sticks like glue. Gripping the centaur's big ears, he tugs them hard and to his amazement Hippodrax staggers to a halt and slowly sinks to his knees. Josh instantly leaps off his shoulders and tensely waits for the next deadly charge ... but nothing happens. The beast lolls on the ground with saliva dripping from his open mouth!

'Hah! I've beaten Hippodrax!'

Suddenly the hold is pushed wide open and Julius calls out.

'Hey, puer – boy!'

As the sailor drops down into the hold, Hippodrax disappears like a dark vapour. Julius gapes at Josh's arms and face, which are slashed and bleeding.

'Eh, what happen?'

Josh shakes his head. How can he begin to explain that a monstrous centaur has been chasing him around the hold for the last quarter of an hour?

'Come. I wash you,' says Julius.

It's only when Josh is up on deck that he realises that the

storm has passed. As Caecilius steers the craft through the warm night, moonlight silvers the waves lapping against the prow. Julius bathes Josh's wounds then offers him some sweet wine mixed with water.

'Canis, she all right?' he asks.

Josh gasps. How could he have forgotten Muck who was in his pouch throughout the entire fight?

'Oh, no!'

He reaches into the pouch and feels a soft, warm bundle of fur.

'Muck! *Muck!*'

She doesn't stir. Josh gently lifts her out and holds her in his hands. Her eyes are closed and a tiny trickle of blood is oozing from her mouth.

'NO!' he screams and bursts into floods of tears.

Julius takes the pup from him and feels her heartbeat.

'Nearly morte.'

He gently massages her tiny ribcage with his thumb and forefinger.

'Open mouth and breathe for canis!' he commands.

Josh realises he's telling him to give Muck mouth-to-mouth resuscitation. He remembers how they did it on TV and bends over the pup, whose heart is still being massaged by Julius. He opens her little mouth and breathes inside, 'HAHHH!' then he comes up for air, which he breathes into her again. In and out, in and out ... *don't die, Muck, please don't die*, he prays. In, out, in, out – then she moves!

'VIVIT! She lives!' cry the sailors in delight. Muck's

bemused eyes light on her master, who bursts into tears for the second time in five minutes!

'Oh, Muck,' he sobs. 'Don't go and die on me again!'

Josh stays on deck with the sailors, who find some fresh water for Muck and a tasty sardine, which she wolfs back.

'You've just been to the edge of the grave and you're eating like a horse!' laughs Josh as he watches her devour the food with a mixture of pride and relief. He makes a bed for her on deck then curls up beside her until she drops off to sleep. As the pup snores gently by his side, Josh stares up at the myriad stars and makes out the constellation that is Perseus. He thinks of his friend Heracles, who has just saved his life by giving him the strength to fight off Hippodrax.

'I miss you …' he whispers.

A falling star flashes across the heavens then disappears down beyond the pale horizon. As dawn breaks on a new day in Ancient Greece, Josh wonders if Heracles has finally found peace.

The weather stays fine over the next few days and Joshua remains on deck with the sailors, playing his lyre to accompany their jolly songs. As the boat skims across the bouncing waves, Caecilius waves a hand towards the west, where a fringe of land is barely discernible.

'Sicilia – home!' he yells excitedly.

'Where go *you*?' asks Julius.

'To meet my father.'

The two men nod in approval.

'Pater … good.'

Josh doesn't like to add that he's meeting his father on the dark side of hell! He stares out across the ocean and sees a tiny speck, which grows bigger and bigger as it approaches the boat. Josh suddenly sees the speck has wings – it's Mate! Julius grins and points at the seagull.

'Big bird for dinner!'

'NO!' cries Josh indignantly. 'Big bird *my friend*!'

Mate lands on the mast and beadily eyes the two sailors gazing curiously up at him.

'It's OK,' Josh calls out, 'I've told them to lay off.'

'RAWK!' goes Mate as he swoops down and lands on his shoulder.

'Big bird like you!' cries Julius in surprise.

'I like him too!' laughs Josh as Mate affectionately tweaks his ear lobe.

All of a sudden, Caecilius leaps to his feet and points to a growing mass of black cloud on the horizon.

'Poseidon come again! He *VERY* angry!'

Josh's heart sinks. Can the Sea God be even angrier than he was before? Can this storm possibly be *worse* than the last one?

'Go down!' Caecilius tells him.

Josh shakes his head. He doesn't want to go below and sit in the dark hold where Leirtod might be waiting for him. He prefers to be on deck with the sailors, who are busily battening everything down. As the wind gets up, Julius secures the flapping mast and Caecilius takes a firm hold of the tiller. Joshua tucks Muck into her pouch and pats her gently on the head.

'Sorry girl, you're in for a soaking.'

The wind has whipped the clouds into a dark, swirling vortex, which dances across the water straight towards them.

'HOLD TIGHT!' yells Caecilius over the screaming noise of the vortex, which hits the craft full on. Mate screeches and flaps his wings but his webbed feet remain firmly planted on Josh's shoulder as the boat spins across the ocean like a whirling top! Joshua can see nothing but a huge wall of water, which towers higher and higher then smashes down, totally submerging the boat. Mate flies up as Josh is thrown overboard. His sailor friends reach out to grab his grasping hands but a great surge snatches him away and drags him down … down … down.

As the air bubbles out of his lungs, Josh sees Leirtod's pale face grinning up at him from the seabed, which is littered with the bleached skeletons of long-dead men and women. With all his strength Josh flings himself up. 'I'm not going to die!' he screams inside his head. He strikes out with his arms and legs, kicking and pushing himself towards the surface of the water, where a pale light glimmers. He bobs up like a cork and gasps in great mouthfuls of air. Simultaneously he reaches into his pouch for Muck, who he lifts clear of the water so that she too can breathe.

He looks around for the boat … the vortex has passed and taken the boat and the sailors with it. Joshua is *all* alone … Well, not quite all alone.

'AWWWWK!'

Mate is circling over his head. He dips a wing, indicating land to the left. Josh yells.

'What about Muck?'

The gull plummets down and picks up the struggling pup in his bright-yellow beak. Muck yaps and wriggles in terror, but Mate holds on tight and swerves off towards the nearby shore. Led as much by Muck's squeals as by Mate, Josh swims after them as quickly as he can.

'Ruff! Ruff!' Mate barks impatiently from the shore.

Gasping for breath, Josh staggers out of the shallows and looks around at the wild coastline, which is fringed with dark poplar trees and willows. He shivers – it's a bleak, hostile coast, but at least it's LAND!

'AWWK!'

Josh spots Mate perched on a high rocky crag with Muck at his feet.

'I'm coming!' he calls, over a roaring sound which shakes the rock under his feet. Whining with relief, Muck scampers forwards and leaps into his arms.

'You're safe now,' Josh assures her as he tucks her into her pouch, but his words are drowned out by the deafening thunder.

'What is that noise?' mutters Josh.

He warily edges his way to the top of the crag and peeps

over. The sight that meets his eyes causes his heart to skip a beat – in a deep gorge far below, two foaming rivers converge with furious impact.

'Could these be the River of Flaming Fire and the River of Lamentation that Heracles told me about?' he murmurs in awe.

'RAWK!' squawks Mate.

Josh looks at the bird, who vehemently nods his head.

'Is this the entrance to the Underworld?'

The bird flies off and lands beside a cave, which he waddles into. Josh runs after him, with Heracles' words echoing inside his head: 'Enter the cave hung with shimmering stone and follow the steep path which will lead you down to the dark waters of the Styx.'

His blood runs cold. Has he finally reached his destination?

'Mate … ?' he calls as he nervously enters the huge cavern.

Mate … Mate … Mate … his voice echoes around the shimmering stone walls.

'*AWWWK! AWWWK! AWWWK!*' the bird echoes back.

Josh looks around and locates Mate at the mouth of a rocky descent, which is so steep it seems to cut into the bowels of the earth. His pulse quickens and he begins to tremble as he realises what he has to do. His instinct is to run out of the cave into the warm light of day, but how many people would he fail if he turned and walked away?

172

How many precious gifts would he waste simply because he was *scared*? He *must* follow this path to his destiny. His friends are not beside him, holding his hands, but they are with him, supporting him. He has Heracles' strength, Athene's wisdom, Zeus's protection, Apollo's lyre, Tiresias's knowledge – and above all else, Lumaluce's love. Strengthened by the gifts of the Immortals, Josh takes a deep breath and sets off down the road to hell!

CHAPTER FIFTEEN

The Road to Hell!

As Josh walks underground all sounds fade. The silence is stifling. Mate's screeches frequently shatter the stillness as he warns of every treacherous twist and turn ahead. Josh gets the shock of his life when the path suddenly disappears and in its place is a narrow rocky ledge overhanging an abyss! He forces himself not to panic, reasoning quite sensibly that it's wide enough to walk across – as long as you don't look down! He reassures himself by recalling a game called 'Sharks' that they often played during P. E. lessons. The rule was that they could only walk on the benches, which were 'land'. The floor was the sea. If they fell off the benches into the sea, they were promptly eaten by sharks and were out of the game. The only problem was that the benches were turned *upside down* so the area they walked on was very, *very* narrow. It had been a running joke between him, Dido and Steve which of them could fall into the sea the most. Losing his balance in this situation certainly wouldn't be one bit funny!

Mate waits for him, but he's not squawking impatiently anymore – he seems to sense Josh's hesitancy. The bird waddles along the ledge then turns to Josh and cocks his head to one side, as if to say, 'Come on, it's OK!' Taking his time and concentrating on putting one foot very carefully in front of the other, Josh follows. Mate takes a sharp right-hand turn ... Josh waits for him to squawk or screech a warning but the bird does neither. Assuming that it's safe, he takes the turns and comes face to face with Leirtod, who is dangling Mate limply from one of his hands.

'Your bird friend is a little dazed from a blow on the head I dealt him. Say goodbye to your guide!' he chuckles, as he hurls the bird into the abyss.

'NO!' screams Josh. *NO! ... NO! ... NO!* his horrified echo comes ringing back.

'I wouldn't get too upset,' sneers Leirtod, 'You'll soon be joining him.'

Fear engulfs Joshua, who starts to shake all over. Recalling Athene's words he forces himself to *think*. How can he get away from his enemy? He can't go forwards because Leirtod's standing right in front of him, and he can't go backwards because there's a rock face behind him!

'I have to confess at being surprised you got so far,' says Leirtod mockingly. 'Actually I'm rather pleased. After I've slit your throat, I'll just roll you over the edge and you'll join the other corpses down below on the banks of the Styx. Very convenient for the afterlife, wouldn't you say?'

'What will you do when I'm dead?'

Bold, fearless words burst out of Josh's mouth, contradicting the terror that grips him.

The question seems to amuse Leirtod.

'Mmm, first I shall delight in watching your father weep. I shall savour every moment of his grief, which I will add to by reminding him how well I became acquainted with you on your journey to meet him.'

As Leirtod goes into vicious detail, Josh sees that there's a slight space between the rock face and his enemy. Can he dash past Leirtod without being grabbed and thrown over the side?

'I shall tell him that you have the same qualities that he had as a boy, the very qualities I admired so much – that should bring scalding tears of agony to his eyes. Oh, I shall delight in Lumaluce's grief,' gloats Leirtod.

Joshua decides it's either death by Leirtod or death by falling into the abyss. If he's to outwit him he *must* keep Leirtod talking; he must keep him off his guard.

'Will my death make you quits with him?'

'Hahhh! Such naivety! Nothing will balance out what I have lost.' As he speaks, Leirtod furiously waves his arms in the air. Every time he lifts them, he frees up a bit more space for Josh to run through.

'*Nothing* will compensate for the thousands of years I have spent in the darkness—'

Josh takes a deep breath and waits for the next arm movement –

NOW!

He darts past Leirtod who makes a grab for his head. He can feel the hairs on his scalp being ripped out, but he keeps on running.

'It'll be worse if you run from me!' screams Leirtod, who is hot on his heels.

Josh nearly laughs out loud! WHAT could be worse than running along a ledge that's crumbling under your feet with a demon on your tail?

Suddenly Josh realises from the sound of Leirtod's footsteps that he's put some distance between himself and his pursuer. Just as things are looking a tad less than terrible, the ledge disappears! He has nowhere to go. Think, lad! He chides himself. *What would you do if you were on a football field surrounded by the opposition with no backup in sight? You know you'd clear the ball somehow! If you can get a ball out from between eleven pairs of kicking legs, you can get yourself out of this situation.*

Steadying his frantic breathing, Josh looks around … his only option is to go up, so he starts to scale the rock face. By the time Leirtod arrives at the spot where the ledge stops, Josh is a good two metres up above him, clinging to the rock like a limpet! Leirtod's evil laughter rings around the cave.

'Oh Hippodrax, you have a visitor coming to see you!'

Clattering hooves on the ledge less than a metre above Joshua's head send sharp stones rolling into his face. He splutters as Hippodrax peers down and breathes his rancid breath into his upturned face.

'What do you think, beast – can you kick him to his death from there?'

Joshua closes his eyes, convinced that his end is imminent.

'Oh, Athene, please give me bucketloads of wisdom!' he implores.

'THINK!' her voice sings out inside his head. 'Be as wise as your father.'

He thinks, fast! *I can't go up or down. Maybe I should try going sideways!* Clinging to every hand and foothold he scuttles sideways across the rock face, then to his utter amazement he tumbles into a hole. It's an owl's eyrie! The big snowy owl that he's disturbed wakes with a screech and bites his nose, then flies off, leaving him surrounded by feathers and stinking owl pellets. Josh crouches down in the hole and listens to Hippodrax angrily stamping the rock above his head. He wonders how long he can stay there before the owl comes back and gives him another painful bite. He looks under the nest and discovers that it's perched on the top of what looks like a narrow tunnel. Quickly pushing the nest to one side, Josh enters the tunnel, which is a tight fit – especially with the lyre strung across his back. He eases the instrument round to the front so that it's lying across his chest and lifts Muck from her pouch so that she won't get squashed to death.

'Breathe in,' he tells her as he slithers down the tunnel, which slowly opens out. Sighing with relief Josh stretches his arms and legs, but suddenly the tunnel disappears and he's left grasping nothing but fresh air.

Thinking he's falling into an abyss Josh screams at the

top of his voice, but his fall is not a long one. He's surprised and relieved when he hits the ground and finds himself back on the steep descending path. Clutching the lyre he stuffs startled Muck back into her pouch and sets off running. That scream of his was loud enough to alert Leirtod to his whereabouts – he and Hippodrax are bound to be on his heels in no time at all. Joshua runs like he's never run before or will ever run again. He feels as though he has the wings of Hermes on his feet as he leaps down the path with his feet hardly touching the ground. And then he hears Hippodrax's galloping feet.

'Get him before he reaches the Styx!' screams Leirtod.

With stones clattering and rolling underfoot, Josh flies down the track with Hippodrax breathing down his neck, his foetid breath almost stifling him. Suddenly he hears a trickle of water, which grows stronger and louder. It's the River Styx – he's nearly there! With his lungs bursting, Josh breaks into a sprint – the sort Stavros would be proud of – and reaches the banks of the river, which he leaps into. Shocked by the impact of the water, Muck scrambles out of her pouch and claws her way up to his chest, where she sits shivering, with her head just above water level.

'Shhh!' Josh whispers in her ear.

Wiping water off his face he looks around and sees Hippodrax and Leirtod standing on the riverbank, staring at him. Why don't they wade in after him? Then he realises that they're *not* looking at him … they're looking past him, across the Styx to an old man standing by the gates of the

Underworld. His heart leaps with joy – Tiresias! It seems like a lifetime ago that the blind seer set him off on his quest. Leirtod is yelling at the old man.

'Give the boy to me!' he bellows.

Unruffled by his bullying tactics the Seer calmly answers.

'No. You have failed to claim him.'

Leirtod flays at the air and screams in fury.

'I will have Lumaluce's son!'

He runs towards Josh, but as his feet touch the water Tiresias holds up his arms and Leirtod stops dead in his tracks, as if frozen.

'Do not enter hallowed ground!'

'Give him to me!'

Suddenly a thousand angry voices fill the air. Hippodrax squeals, then rears and gallops back up the path, neighing in terror. The angry whispers get louder and turn rapidly into shrieks of deranged frenzy.

'*AAAAAAAAAAHHHH!*'

'THE FURIES!' screams Leirtod.

The Furies appear, three winged grey shadows, with crawling snakes wreathed around their heads. They whine and howl until their combined voices reach an echoing crescendo. There is a sob as they uniformly inhale, then their voices come raging back, louder and more tormented than before. Joshua stands in the Styx, rooted to the spot with terror, but Leirtod is in *agony*! He covers his ears, trying to block out their cries.

'Tell them to stop – make them go away,' he pleads.

'The Furies will only stop when they have exacted vengeance for your acts of violence,' Tiresias tells him.

Leirtod glares at Joshua crouching in the shallows. He reaches into the folds of his cloak – Josh knows *exactly* what he's reaching for.

'Shed no blood in the resting place of the dead!' Tiresias commands.

The Furies increase their crying to a high-pitched howl which sends Leirtod into a ranting, raging madness.

'STOP! Oh, please stop!' he begs.

'They will hound you!' Tiresias screams over the eerie howling of the Furies. 'You must leave this place before they take their vengeance.'

Leirtod turns to Josh, his face as white as marble, his eyes burning with hatred.

'One day, son of Lumaluce, I will have my revenge!' he vows, and with a swirl of his billowing cloak he melts away into the darkness.

As the presence of evil fades, the Furies' spectral, shadowy shapes recede. The only sound remaining is from the slow, lapping waters of the Styx.

Joshua staggers exhausted on to the riverbank, where he slumps down, unable to believe that Leirtod is gone.

'Why did he run away?' he asks Tiresias.

'He's terrified of the Furies.'

'Who are they?'

'They are the Goddesses of Retribution,' the old seer

replies. 'They exact punishment for murder, especially from those who have murdered their families – a crime that Leirtod is guilty of. They mercilessly pursue their culprits and hound them into madness with their cries.'

'Will they kill Leirtod?' Josh asks hopefully.

'No, they cannot kill him, but they can make him suffer more than any other thing on earth.'

'Good!' laughs Josh with real delight. 'I'm thrilled they turned up!'

'They constantly pursue Leirtod for his crimes but he cunningly eludes them.'

Joshua starts in fear as he feels a rush of wind behind his back. He blinks in amazement when he finds the Winged Messenger God standing on the riverbank.

'Hermes! What are you doing here?'

Hermes raps him impatiently with his Moly stick.

'Haven't you forgotten something, mortal fool?'

Josh looks up at him, stupefied.

'Forgive me, great god, my brain's a bit addled by the screams of the Furies!'

'Oh, those three noisy old bags!' Hermes replies dismissively.

'I liked them!' Joshua tells him.

'Ooooo!' mocks Hermes, 'You must be the only mortal in history who's a fan of the Furies!'

'They saved my life,' Joshua tells him.

'Somebody is always saving your wretched little life,' Hermes snaps. 'This time it's me. Athene sent me to remind you of **THE SACRIFICE.**'

Josh claps a hand to his mouth as he recalls Heracles' instructions: *Before you enter Hades you must dig a trench as long and wide as your forearm, then go around the trench and pour in sweet wine, honey, milk and water. Sprinkle over this the white barley and pray for the souls of the dead. Then you must sacrifice a ram and a black ewe and pour their blood into the ground.*

'Hahh! I've forgotten the ram and the ewe and the—'

'You've forgotten *everything.*'

'I've got the white barley and a coin to pay the ferryman,' Joshua says in his own defence.

'And what about the rest?'

'I didn't think of them when I entered the Underworld!'

'FOOL!'

'Where would I find a ram and a black ewe at the place where the Rivers of Fire and Lamentation meet?' Josh asks.

'You were given good warning and clear advice on what to do,' says Hermes spitefully.

'Don't make me go all the way back!' Josh implores.

'You don't have to!'

Hermes clicks his fingers and there before him stands a ram and a black ewe.

'You *do* remember what you have to do, don't you?' he enquires crossly.

Josh nods.

'First I have to dig a trench as long and wide as my forearm then go around the trench and pour in offerings of sweet wine, honey, milk, water …' His voice trails away. 'I haven't got any of those things either,' he admits.

Hermes looks like he could boil him in hot olive oil!

'Oh, you *do* surprise me! One day I will ask Athene why she indulges you, because right now I am at a loss to understand it!'

'Oh, p-l-e-a-s-e, Hermes …' Josh implores.

The Winged Messenger irritably snaps his fingers and little bowls of milk, wine, honey and water appear on the riverbank.

'Now get on with it!'

With his bare hands, scrapes a small hollow the same length and width as his forearm. Then, taking up each bowl in turn, he goes round the trench, pouring in first the wine, then the water, the milk, and last the honey. He shakes the white barley out of the purse that Tiresias gave him at the start of his journey. As the barley mixes with the other offerings, he prays for the souls of the dead. His prayers are rudely interrupted by Hermes giving him a jab in the ribs.

'You're forgetting something.' He nods towards the ram and the black ewe. 'Slaughter them.'

Josh looks into their trusting dark eyes and shakes his head.

'I can't!'

Hermes turns his eyes upwards. 'The Gods give me patience with this mortal idiot!' He pauses, as if to steady his temper. 'It is not a question of choice – you have to do it. The sacrifice *has* to be made to Hades and Persephone or you will not be allowed entry into the Underworld. Heracles gave you his knife – use it!'

'I've never killed anything in my life.'

'If you want to see Lumaluce you'd better start *now*.'

Joshua takes Heracles' knife from the scabbard and fiddles with it nervously. Hermes gives him a shove.

'Stand behind their heads, dig the blade deep in to the windpipe and CUT!'

Josh grits his teeth and takes a deep breath, then crosses to the ram, which bleats in fear. Grabbing it firmly around the neck, he tips its head backwards and jabs the knife deep into its throat. The blood spurts out in a fountain, splattering his hair and face. The ram staggers, then falls over on to its side, with blood gushing in torrents from the gaping wound that was its neck. Josh immediately turns to the ewe, but smelling blood she panics and tries to run. He throws himself on to her. She struggles and bleats pathetically, but Joshua pulls her head hard back and performs the grim slaughter one more time. Feeling sick to his stomach, he soaks the ground in their hot, red blood then turns to Hermes, who has vanished into thin air!

'I have completed my sacrifice,' he calls out to Tiresias.

'Persephone and Hades are pleased with your libations. They allow you entry into their kingdom.'

Josh gasps with relief and immediately starts to walk into the river.

'NO! You can only cross with Charon the Ferryman,' Tiresias calls. 'Find him and see if he will bring you over.'

'Don't forget to give him a coin,' invisible Hermes whispers. 'He won't give you a free ride!'

CHAPTER SIXTEEN

The Fields of Joy

'AAWWK!' Josh laughs with relief when he sees Mate waddling along the banks of the River Styx towards him.

'Oh, Mate, I thought you were dead!'

The seagull cocks his head to one side and gives him a beady stare as if to say, 'ME? I'm *indestructible!*' At the sound of the gull, Muck pops out of her pouch and yaps hungrily.

'Forget it, Muck,' says Josh. 'This is the place of the dead and believe me, they don't eat!'

Whining in disappointment Muck wriggles back down into her pouch and Josh hurries after Mate, who is flying over weeping-willow trees that shed their seeds on to the bank. Suddenly the stench of steaming sulphur stings the back of his nostrils.

'UGHHH!' he gags as he lifts the bottom of his tunic to cover his nose. 'What IS that smell?'

The ground under his feet turns black and soggy. Mud sticks to his bare feet, hampering his hurrying footsteps. The mud covers a stinking, deep sludge which Joshua has to wade chest-deep through. Just as he's beginning to think he might be swallowed up in the sulphurous swamp, Mate squawks and a hand appears before his face. He jumps in fear – is it Leirtod returning to finish him off? Cautiously he looks up and gazes into the face of a filthy, stinking old man with long white hair and a dirty grey beard that straggles down to his waist. He looks as old as time, but his eyes burn like points of bright light. He grabs Josh's hand and yanks him out of the foul mud, then dumps him back on to the riverbank, which is crowded with pale ghostly shadows.

Josh stares in horror at the line-up of the dead. Mothers, babies, toddlers, boys and girls younger than himself, all queuing up to cross the River Styx. He shudders and quickly backs away, but in his haste he bumps into another crowd of ghosts, all of who are men. Suddenly he recognises the Italian sailors, Caecilius and Julius. He tries to grab hold of them but his hand grasps at nothing. He looks into their dead eyes, which are nothing now but gaping, blank sockets.

'They were my friends!' he cries out to the boatman.

Charon shrugs.

'Now they join the ranks of the dead.'

Josh cannot take his eyes off the sailors who he met in Piraeus harbour. Only days ago they were strong and healthy, happy to be going home – they were kind to him. Now they are grey and motionless.

Charon boards the ferry and starts to push against the bank with a long wooden punt pole.

'STOP! Don't leave my friends!'

The ferryman shakes his head. 'Their time has not yet come.'

'But they're dead!' Joshua protests. 'Just like the corpses on your boat.'

'They died by accident,' the boatman replies. 'The savage elements claimed them, not the gods.'

Joshua is appalled. 'When will you take them to the Underworld?'

'When their allotted time comes round.'

'What does that mean?' cries Josh in frustration.

'When they reach the age they *should* have died I will ferry them across the river of death,' the boatman replies as he pushes off.

Joshua watches the wake of water disappear behind the laden boat, then all sounds fade. He is surrounded by a deathly stillness that chills him to the bone. He doesn't want to look into the faces of his dead companions, but he is mesmerised by them, all of them – men, women, children and tiny babies. Their shadows crowd the banks waiting for the gods to grant them the right of entry into the afterlife.

'I'll pray for you all if I ever get out of here,' he promises.

Through the cloying gloom he hears the regular splash of Charon's pole as he plies his way back across the stretch of water. Josh leaps to his feet and cries out.

'Charon! I have a penny to pay my fare. Will you take me next?'

'You can't travel with me. You're alive, boy.'

'But I have to go to the Underworld – I *need* to go,' Josh pleads.

'Your time will come,' says Charon as he drifts into the bank and disembarks in order to start loading up again.

As Charon heaps the bodies of small children into the stern, Joshua suddenly remembers how Orpheus charmed him. He takes his lyre from around his shoulders and gently strums it.

'Please, Apollo, bless my song,' he prays silently.

When he opens his mouth to sing he's startled by the loveliness of his voice. He's *never* in all his life sung like this before! Charon smiles and closes his eyes as the wonderful harmonies echo up and down the banks of the Styx. When the music fades away, Charon extends a hand to Joshua.

'Give me your coin then help me load my cargo. I will take you over, mortal, but I cannot promise to bring you back,' he warns.

Joshua nods and between them they heap dozens of corpses into the boat, which finally lurches out across the murky waters of the River Styx.

When they land on the other side, Charon clambers ashore and starts to haul the boat in. Suddenly the dank air is filled with horrific blood-curdling howls that cause Joshua's hair to stand on end.

'What's *that*?'

'Cerberus, the Hound from Hell!'

The howls grow louder and angrier, and a monstrous three-headed dog explodes out of the gates of the Underworld. A mane of snakes bristles and writhes around his three heads, which seem to turn in all directions. His hackles rise and he drools from his three great mouths as he smells the red blood of a living, breathing thing.

'Do something quickly, boy, or the hound will eat you alive!' warns Charon.

Suddenly the strings of Apollo's lyre strum. Josh stares at them in disbelief – *he* never touched them! He recognises the tune – it's Jimi Hendrix's 'Wild Thing', the song he sang in the cell with Pythagoras. Apollo is reminding him how to charm the dog! Jumping up, he twangs the lyre as loudly as he can and sings at the top of his voice.

'WILD THING! You make my heart sing!'

Jumping and gyrating, he dances around Cerberus, who slavers and drools from his three foul-smelling mouths. Josh sings and dances until his voice turns into a hoarse croak and he is forced to stop. He warily watches Cerberus ... will he devour him or let him pass? The hound moves away from his guard-post. Josh dashes past him and runs as fast as he can, just in case Cerberus changes his mind! He's running so fast he runs slap-bang into Tiresias, who is waiting for him.

'Hah!'

'You have come far, Joshua Cross,' says the seer.

'My journey is completed, Tiresias,' he says boldly. 'Where is my father?'

'He is waiting for you.'

With his heart banging against his ribcage, Joshua follows in the seer's footsteps. Will his father like him? *Everybody* he's met on his journey told him what a great man he is, a superhero – a Legend. Is he worthy enough to be Luma-luce's son? His anxious thoughts are interrupted by the cries of dead men stretched out on large wooden racks.

'What are they doing?' asks Josh.

'They are paying retribution – purging themselves of their sins.'

'How?'

'Their souls are stretched out for the wind to blow away their offences,' the seer replies. 'Others are washed in the sea of purification, some are burnt clean by fire. When they are without taint and have been made as pure and bright as a spark of elemental fire, they will find peace in the Underworld.'

'When I first met you on the island of Zachynthus you told me that my father lived in the Fields of Joy beyond Hades.'

'I am taking you to the place where the Legends dwell.'

Shaking in every limb, Joshua follows Tiresias through Hades, which is a place of misty plains and sad, drooping trees with branches that sweep the ground and sigh dismally as they pass by. The wind-swept plains give way to green, rolling fields and the pool of Lethe, which Tiresias forbids him to drink from.

'One sip and you will immediately forget your former life in the world above,' he warns.

Beyond the pool rise the towers of Persephone and Hades' palace where the shades of the dead are judged by the King and Queen of the Underworld.

'Quickly, boy, follow me,' Tiresias says as he takes a grassy track that takes them beyond the gloomy palace. 'See how little worn this path is,' he points out. 'Only the few who are blessed by the Immortals tread this way.'

The Fields of Joy await them ... a heavenly place where the sun shines and the only clouds in the sky are white and fleecy. Birds sing out from the treetops and all around them is the sweet music of the pipes and the lyre.

In a sunlit grove dappled with wild flowers, a tall man stands waiting for them. He is wearing silver armour, which catches the light and dazzles Joshua with its brilliance. He blinks and covers his eyes.

When he opens them he is gazing into the eyes of his father ... eyes as silvery bright as his own. Lumaluce lays a hand upon his head and Joshua feels a huge wave of love flow through his body, a love so sweet and intense it makes him smile with joy. Lumaluce takes him into his arms and holds him close.

'Here is my one true son,' he says as tears course down his face and drop on to Joshua's tangled hair.

They sit in the grove with wild flowers at their feet and birds singing sweetly overhead.

'I feel like I've died and gone to heaven!' says Josh.

'You are in heaven – but you haven't died!'

'Can I stay with you?'

Lumaluce shakes his head.

'Not yet.'

'*Please* let me stay,' he begs.

Lumaluce puts an arm around his shoulder and draws him close.

'Joshua, you have a long life before you.'

Joshua wriggles uncomfortably as he forces himself to ask the question that's been nagging him since he was whisked away from Shakespeare's Chippy.

'I know you're my dad and I know why Leirtod hates you and tries to kill me. I know you're a timeless Legend loved by the gods. What I don't know is why *I'm* in danger and not Tom. He is your son too, isn't he?'

'Yes, he is my son …' Lumaluce falters briefly, then adds. 'Joshua, you must realise that I have fathered many children over the centuries.'

'So you must have had other wives and partners as well as mum?'

Lumaluce nods.

'But not *all* at the same time!' he says with a gentle smile.

'I hope my mum was the best,' Josh says with an edge to his voice.

'Your mother is wonderful,' Lumaluce assures him. 'I was taken from her when our love was young, but she lives for ever in my heart.'

'She never re-married,' Josh tells him. 'Even though the pie man has fancied her for years.'

'I'd strike him down and roast him on a thunderbolt wrought by Zeus if he as much as laid a finger on my lady!'

Having established that his mum's the best woman *ever* to have been born, Josh moves on to the question of why he is the most troubled of his sons.

'If you've got other kids, why doesn't Leirtod try to kill them too?'

'He's interested in you because you inherited my spirit.'

'And he'll get his revenge on you through killing me,' Josh adds. 'He told me that himself, in the prison cell in Athens.'

'I have been proud of you my son. You have fought hard and survived much.' He pauses to stroke his son's pale cheek. 'He will continue to track you down, but this quest through Ancient Greece has given you great knowledge. You now have tools to fight Leirtod – wisdom, strength, cunning, courage. You have gathered a knowledge of him and of his weaknesses.'

'He's scared stiff of the Furies!'

'That knowledge might one day save your life.'

'But I can't be on the run forever!' Joshua exclaims. 'I don't want to stay in Ancient Greece – I need to look after mum!'

'Don't worry, Joshua, I shall return you to the future. I too want you to take care of my beloved lady. Listen to me, child,' he adds solemnly. 'In the future you will be vulnerable. In the years between now and your manhood, Leirtod can take you. But with every passing year your strength and wisdom will grow, until finally you will surpass his evil forces.'

'I'll be stronger than Leirtod?' Josh asks incredulously.

'Of course. You have legendary stock in your blood.'

'You mean I could be a Legend like *you*?'

'Oh, yes, *if* you live to manhood,' Lumaluce replies grimly. 'But remember – Leirtod will not give up until he is forced to.'

'I'm scared of him, dad!'

'You should be scared of him! He is evil.'

'I can't fight him on my own.'

'You already have, Joshua! And though you may not see me, I will always be at your side.'

'Will Leirtod be able to find me wherever I go?'

'He'll try to find you, but he may not succeed. You beat him this time, my son! You will surely beat him again.'

'What will I tell mum when I get back? She'll have half the London Police Force out looking for me.'

'Your journey in Ancient Greece happened outside your life in the twenty-first century. *Nothing* changed there.'

Tiresias shuffles towards them and looks with his unseeing eyes into Lumaluce's face.

'The boy's time is up, my lord Lumaluce. The gods allowed him entry to the Fields of Joy because of their love for you. He must not outstay his allotted span.'

Tears sting the back of Josh's eyes. 'No! I don't want to go!'

Lumaluce holds him close. 'Now that you've found me, we'll always be together.'

Joshua clings to him, stifling his sobs. 'I love you, dad!'

'And I love you, Joshua Cross. We share one spirit, fused for all eternity.' His father takes a deep breath to steady himself. 'Take him, Heracles, before my strength fails me.'

'HERACLES!'

Josh whirls around and sees that Tiresias has been replaced by Heracles.

'You're *here!*' he gasps.

Heracles smiles and nods. 'Yes, Joshua. I live with the Legends now.'

Light blazes off his father's breastplate, drenching Joshua in its warmth. Lumaluce raises his right hand in a final salute. 'Goodbye, my son!' he calls, and then the light is gone.

'Dad … ?' calls Josh on the edge of tears.

Heracles puts a comforting arm around Josh. 'Come,' he says firmly.

He leads him out of the Fields of Joy, back through Hades, where the souls of the dead continue to chant their prayers of retribution, and out of the gates of the Underworld. On the murky banks of the River Styx, Cerberus growls at him from his three slobbering mouths.

'It's time to go home, Joshua,' says Heracles.

'B … but …'

'The gods will protect you. Farewell little Hyperborean – I will never forget you!'

With these words he turns his back and re-enters the Underworld.

'*How* am I going to get back home?' Josh cries after him.

'AWWWK!'

The seagull waddles towards him.

'Mate! You'll guide me.'

'That could take a *very long* time!' a familiar, irritable voice snaps behind him.

'Hermes!'

'Yes, me,' he replies wearily. 'Athene has instructed me to take you back to that far-flung, freezing island south of Hyperborea that you inhabit.'

'It's called *England*.'

Hermes isn't listening. He's intent on attaching little golden wings to Joshua's ankles.

'This is so c-o-o-o-l!' giggles Josh as he flutters up into the air.

'Not if you do it all the time,' answers Hermes.

'AWWK!' goes Mate.

'Is *he* coming too?' the god asks.

Joshua opens his mouth to say yes, but the seagull screeches and cocks his head to one side.

'I take that as a yes,' says Hermes. 'Just stay out of my way bird – it's a long journey north and I don't want YOU under my feet!'

Muck pops out of her pouch and yelps excitedly.

'That too?' snaps Hermes as he points at the pup.

'Of course!' Josh tells him.

'Is there anything else you'd like to take back?' Hermes

asks sarcastically. 'A mountain goat from Arcadia, a chunk of the Parthenon, perhaps a bottle of water from the River Styx?'

'Just my friends, Muck and Mate,' Josh laughs.

Hermes impatiently whooshes off. 'Come on, mortal, let's not hang about!'

They fly high over Charon loading his ferry, then up the treacherously steep path that Joshua has only recently raced down, pursued by Hippodrax. As they emerge from the bowels of the earth, Joshua is dazzled by the bright sunlight. They skim over the sparkling-blue Mediterranean, passing shoals of leaping dolphins, then they take a sharp right-hand turn. As they fly north, the sun disappears behind dark storm clouds. Hermes scowls as raindrops spatter his bare chest.

'WHY do mortals choose to live so far north?' he grumbles.

Joshua smiles. He doesn't mind the weather – it feels like home!

They cross the churning, grey English Channel then zip up the River Thames from Gravesend. The miles fly by and so do the centuries as they flash by the familiar London landmarks – Cleopatra's Needle, Westminster Abbey, the Tower of London, the Globe, the Houses of Parliament, St Paul's Cathedral, Big Ben, Waterloo Station, Westminster Bridge, St Thomas's Hospital – HOME! Joshua can smell home well before he sees it. The aroma of frying fish and chips drifts towards him on the cold north wind.

'I live there!' he tells Hermes as he points to Shakespeare's Chippy down below.

The Winged Messenger flutters in mid-air. 'The son of Lumaluce lives in a fish shop!'

'It's the best chip shop in London,' Joshua tells him proudly.

'I beg you, boy, don't ask me to sample the goods. Fish makes me sick – it reminds me of my grumpy Uncle Poseidon!'

They land on the banks of the River Thames, where Hermes says a curt goodbye.

'If you're ever near Mount Olympus, *please* don't look me up, Joshua Cross!'

And with that, he's gone … flitting home to Mount Olympus to join the Immortals in the everlasting sunshine. Joshua sighs, torn between a huge longing to go back and a great desire to stay. Mate squawks and leads Josh along the wharf to Shakespeare's Chippy, where he flies up on to the boy's shoulder.

'It's time for you to leave me too, isn't it, old friend?'

Mate nibbles his ear and cackles affectionately, then flies up and circles the air above his head. He swerves on the breeze to look back at Josh, then he swoops off down the Thames and out to sea. Seeing him go brings a rush of tears to Josh's eyes. Will he ever see his guide again?

He pushes open the shop door. Mrs Cross is there, swirling chips in a great fryer of hot oil. She looks up and smiles at her son.

'Hello, love, had a good day at school?'

Joshua nearly laughs out loud. Lumaluce was right – *nothing* has changed for her but *everything* has changed for him. He has been to Ancient Greece and fought with monsters, he has sacrificed beasts and raced in the Olympics, he has seen Legends and sat in the Fields of Joy with his father – and his mother hasn't even noticed him gone!

'Mum, I had the best day *e-v-e-r!*'

Mrs Cross looks surprised.

'That's nice, you don't normally enjoy school.'

'Today was different,' Josh says, and then he asks a question he's never dared to ask.

'Mum, did you love my dad?'

Mrs Cross stares at her youngest son. Her eyes fill with tears as she answers his question.

'Your dad, Joshua, was the most wonderful man that ever lived – a legend. I loved him very, very much ... and I always will.'

Josh smiles knowingly. 'He loves you too, mum!'

Their conversation is interrupted by Muck, who smelling food, wriggles out of her pouch and yaps hungrily.

'Joshua – *where* did you get that dog?' gasps Mrs Cross in amazement.

He chuckles as he tickles Muck's silky little ears.

'Mother, you *really* wouldn't want to know!'

Glossary

A full glossary will appear in the final version of this book.

Joshua Cross and the Legends will be illustrated throughout by Oscar Zarate, who won the Will Eisner Prize for the best graphic novel of 1994.